Cougar Chronicles

Cougar Chronicles

THE COWBOY AND THE COUGAR

CALENDAR BOY

HELEN HARDT

WATERHOUSE PRESS

To all the cougars out there!

TABLE OF CONTENTS

THE COWBOY AND THE COUGAR 7

CALENDAR BOY 135

THE
Cowboy
AND THE COUGAR

CHAPTER ONE

"Sugar, you look like you just lost your best friend."

The voice was deep and husky. Very sexy. Holly Taylor didn't look up from her empty martini glass. She speared the remaining gin-soaked olive with her sword-shaped toothpick, twirled it in the last drop of alcohol, and popped it in her mouth. The piquant saltiness exploded across her tongue. She closed her eyes and inhaled.

She'd get through this. She had no choice.

"What can I get you?"

Holly opened her eyes at the female bartender's squeaky voice. Damned annoying, especially for a swanky hotel bar, but the woman poured a mean martini.

"Scotch, neat," the male voice said, "and another for the lady."

Nope. Not another. Holly was driving. No matter what lay ahead, she couldn't get drunk and drive home. She turned her head to thank the gentleman and met the darkest, smokiest, most beautiful eyes she'd ever seen.

The rest of him wasn't bad, either.

"You okay?" he asked.

Uh, yeah. Her mouth hung open and she quickly shut it. "Thank you, sir"—*Sir? He had to be at least ten years her junior!*—"but I don't want another drink."

His eyes twinkled behind their ebony curtain of lashes. "I'm not sure anyone's ever called me sir, sugar. And you look like you could use another."

Holly stared. She couldn't help it. His eyes weren't his only magnificent feature. His face was perfectly sculpted, with high cheekbones and an aquiline nose. A few days' growth of black beard dusted his strong jaw. Onyx hair fell to his shoulders in thick waves. And what shoulders they were—broad, meaty, and clad in a white western shirt complete with silver snaps. His jeans, hat, and boots completed the picture. Here was a real honest-to-goodness cowboy in the middle of the Livingston Palace bar in Denver.

Gorgeous. Simply gorgeous.

The bartender set down another martini. Holly opened her mouth to speak, but the stud next to her touched her forearm. Sparks crept to her cheeks and warmed them.

"It's okay. I'll take care of you."

Take care of her? She let out a sigh. If only her life were that simple. She fingered the stem of the martini glass with her free hand and looked into his amazing eyes. He smiled. What the heck? Maybe a few minutes in this handsome young man's company would take her mind off her problems.

"Thank you," she said. "I may need to take you up on that."

"Any time, sugar." His lazy half-smile dipped as he picked up his drink with his other hand.

When the tip of his tongue touched the rim of his glass, Holly's pulse lurched. She imagined that pink flesh snaking around a hard nipple. One of *her* hard nipples, both of which currently strained against her bra, aching.

Her companion let out a soft laugh. "You going to drink that? Or just squeeze it till it shatters in your hand?"

Holly looked down at her white-knuckled fingers wringing the glass stem. She exhaled and forced her hand to relax. Lifting the drink to her lips, she said, "Cheers," and gulped the martini.

The gin stung her throat as she set the glass back down on the bar.

She'd had a shit day.

But it was about to get a whole lot better, she hoped.

Her neck chilled, and she inhaled and gathered her courage. "You live around here, cowboy?"

"Not too far. You?"

Not too far. He hadn't asked her name. He was wise to keep the conversation impersonal. No names. That would be best. No ages, either. If this young stud knew she'd just hit forty he'd no doubt run for cover.

"I don't think I'm going home tonight," she said. "I think I feel like a room. A suite maybe. A jacuzzi suite."

The cowboy's full lips curved into a grin, and his fingers tensed on her forearm. "Are you asking for company?"

Holly's heart fluttered, but she steadied herself despite the two martinis. She wasn't drunk. It took more than two drinks to get her tipsy. All signals from the man said go. She hadn't had sex in a while. Damn, had it been two years now?

She was forty. Forty and alone, with no one to hold her and comfort her as she cried about what was to come.

She didn't have to be alone tonight.

Tonight, she could escape, albeit temporarily, and make love to a hot younger man. If he was willing, which he seemed to be.

She pushed her empty martini glass toward the bartender and then covered his hand which still warmed her arm. His hands were as beautifully formed as the rest of him, with long thick fingers that would feel really good in lots of places. The soft hair on his knuckles tickled her.

Why not get straight to the point? She met his dark gaze. "If I *were* asking for company, would you be up for it?"

He downed the rest of his Scotch and smiled. "Can't think of a better way to spend the evening, sugar."

Holly gulped. She was really going to do this. "Do you have protection?"

"I was a boy scout." He leaned toward her, and his warm breath caressed her cheek. "I'm always prepared."

★ ★ ★

She wouldn't tell him her name and didn't want to know his.

She'd touched two slender fingers to his lips when he'd tried to introduce himself. "You're Cowboy to me tonight," she'd said. "And I'm Sugar."

Okay, he'd play along, though he'd insisted on paying for the room. She'd stayed far from the front counter as he reserved the best suite the Livingston had available. She probably didn't want to get curious and peek at the name on his credit card.

Fine. For now. He had every intention of knowing this beauty's name and everything else about her before the night was over. Specifically, he wanted to know what or who put that forlorn look in her beautiful eyes.

His hand to her back, he escorted her into the empty elevator. The doors closed.

And she attacked.

His body slammed against the wall of the elevator, and she cupped either side of his face with her smooth hands. She pulled him toward her luscious red lips.

"Kiss me, cowboy."

She crushed her mouth to his. Though his intent was to play with her a little, hold her off, make her beg, he couldn't resist the temptation of her honeyed mouth. When her tongue touched his, he sucked it between his lips. It was soft. So soft and wet, and she tasted like the martinis she'd drunk. Gin, a touch of vermouth, and some spicy lime. Jack wasn't sure where the lime had come from, but it was the perfect compliment.

Her lush body molded to his, and her bountiful breasts mashed against his chest. She was tall, his sugar. Tall enough that he, at six-three, didn't need to strain his neck to kiss her. The silky fabric that covered her plump tits rubbed against him and ignited his loins.

Hell, his loins had been on fire since he'd first seen her. So beautiful and so sad. He'd wanted to help her, hold her, and take away whatever was hurting her.

If he could do that by fucking her, so be it. Yep, that was him. Jack Sherwood. Altruist.

Fuck.

She grabbed his ass, and any further thoughts of altruism fled his mind.

This was not altruism. This was lust, pure and simple. He wanted her, and clearly the feeling was mutual.

The elevator dinged and opened, and he broke the kiss with a loud smack. Her lips, scarlet and swollen, curved slightly into a shy smile. She met his gaze but then looked away quickly.

"Don't get bashful with me now, sugar," Jack said. "You're one hell of a great kisser."

"Who's bashful?" She met his eyes and her own green orbs smoldered.

He smiled. "My mistake." He pulled her from the elevator, down the hallway to room 1145, and trapped her against the door as he fumbled for the keycard in his pocket. Again, her body felt perfect against his, and his arousal ached in his jeans. He pushed it into her soft belly and arched his eyebrow at her gasp.

"You all right?"

"Yeah, sure, cowboy." She grabbed his ass and pulled him harder against her. "I'm fine."

"Damn, sugar." Fine indeed. His jeans had tightened so much he had a hard time finding the keycard, but he had to find it, and fast. Otherwise he was about to fuck the daylights out of her right there in the hall.

He eased away from her to withdraw the card from his pocket. In a flash, her warm hand was at his crotch, cupping him.

"Ah," he groaned and shut his eyes.

Thank God he'd decided to step into the Livingston bar after his appointment earlier.

This was going to be one hell of a good night.

CHAPTER TWO

The cowboy had her in his arms before they were five feet into the room. He took her hand, drew her close, and pressed his body into hers. Holly slid her fingers up the soft cotton of his shirt, grabbed the collar, and released the snaps one by one. She wanted to hurry, to rip the damned thing off him. But she'd tease a little. Take her time. He smiled—damn, he was gorgeous—as she pulled the shirt from his waistband and pushed it off his broad and beefy shoulders. It landed on the floor with a soft swoosh.

Cowboy trailed one finger over her breasts snug in her green polo shirt. Her nipples tightened when he grazed them.

"Fair is fair, sugar. You need to take this off." He pulled her shirt over her head and his calloused fingertips skimmed the sensitive bare skin of her belly.

She shivered as white heat spread to her limbs. Soon her shirt joined his on the floor.

His chocolate gaze dropped to her breasts. Swollen and ripe, they fought against the lace of her bra. Instead of touching them—to her disappointment—he merely looked and then pulled her into his embrace. He squeezed the cheeks of her ass.

She slid her hands over the hard planes of his chest, through the soft smattering of dark hair, up his sleek golden shoulders, and into his soft, dark waves. She sifted the silky strands through her fingers and thought she'd never felt anything quite so soft, so heavenly.

He lowered his lips to hers. So close, they were, but he didn't kiss her. Not even a centimeter separated them, but he didn't bridge the gap.

The fact that he didn't was incredibly erotic. She'd already kissed him in the elevator, but at this moment, she wanted to kiss him more than she wanted her next breath. He caressed her neck with his long, thick fingers, sending shudders through her which landed between her legs. She tried to press closer, to spear him with her painfully hard nipples. Still he tantalized her, warming her lips with his soft breath.

He trailed his fingers from her neck down her shoulder and eased down one strap of her bra. She closed her eyes as the air hit her turgid nipple. Cowboy moaned, cupped her naked breast, and squeezed, and her nipple hardened even further. Her pussy throbbed. Damn, if he didn't kiss her soon, or touch her nipple...really, it didn't have to be much. A little pinch to the hard bud and she'd explode on the spot. She withdrew from his hypnotic stare and kissed his sculpted shoulder. His skin was warm and slightly salty. Very, very masculine.

She turned in his arms, her back to his chest, and he squeezed her breast again. His other hand slithered down her smooth belly and under the waistband of her stretch capris. Into her panties he went, and his long warm fingers sifted through her curls.

She shuddered when he reached her clit. Slowly, methodically, he stroked her moist folds.

"Mmm, wet sugar," he whispered in her ear.

She nodded, unable to speak. His caresses made her blood boil. She squeezed his sinewy arms, his massive shoulders, and then turned her head and bit his hard flesh.

His groan was her reward.

Enough of him being in control. As much as Holly was enjoying his ministrations, she needed to take charge. If he wouldn't kiss her, wouldn't suck her nipple, she'd show him what a tease she could be.

She turned in his arms and dropped to her knees. Her hands trembling, she unbuckled his belt and unzipped his jeans. He fisted his hands in her long dark hair, but she proceeded slowly, methodically. She'd tease him like he'd teased her.

She grasped the rough denim and pushed it down over his lean, sculpted hips.

Before her stood the most amazing cock she'd ever seen. Long, thick, and golden, it sprang from a thick nest of black curls. So much for teasing. That delicious-looking cock was going in her mouth.

She looked up at him. His eyes pierced her with scalding flames. She smiled and met his gaze. God, he was beautiful. She traced lacy patterns on his thighs and continued to stare at his massive erection. His muscle, his skin, felt glorious to her touch.

"Damn," she said under her breath.

"Hmm? What is it, sugar?"

Had he heard her? Warmth crept to her cheeks, but she steadied herself. Why be embarrassed now? She was staring at his naked cock. Time for embarrassment had definitely gone out the window.

"I'm thinking, cowboy"—she reached upward, pressed her hands to his gorgeous chest, and scraped her fingernails downward—"that I'd really like to suck this beautiful cock."

His groan vibrated against the palms of her hands. Good, good. Right where she wanted him.

"Please," he said. "God, please suck it."

Holly leaned forward and took just the head between her lips. Mmm. Delicious, just as she'd expected. A drop of salty pre-come tantalized her tongue, reminding her of the olives in her martini. She loved olives.

And she loved this cowboy's cock.

He pushed forward and tried to nudge his way farther into her mouth, but she held fast, enjoying the feel of his sensitive head against her lips and tongue. She slurped a little, drew back, and rained tiny kisses to the tip. Mmm.

"Damn, sugar." He bent forward and smashed his mouth to hers in a kiss so raw and untamed, she nearly forgot who she was. His tongue tangled with hers, exploring, possessing.

When he ripped his mouth away, she inhaled a needed breath, and he grabbed her hair and forced her back onto his cock.

"Suck me. Please."

He didn't have to say please. She took him deeply this time, let his knob graze the back of her throat. Then she inched back, let it drop from her mouth, and licked the underside, relishing his moans. He still held her by the hair which—she wasn't sure why—turned her on even more. When she took him in her mouth again, his face twisted into a grimace. She hummed softly, knowing the vibration from her voice would tease him.

"God! If you don't stop that I'm going to come."

Holly backed off. No way. No coming until she'd gotten what she came for—a night of hot, heart-stopping sex. "So good I can't remember my own name" sex. That's what she needed right now.

To forget her own name.

To forget everything.

Cowboy gathered Holly into his arms and carried her to the bedroom. He laid her gently on the bed and quickly disposed of her bra. His eyes widened.

"Damn, sugar, you've got beautiful breasts." He pinched a nipple. "Gorgeous nipples, too. Perfect."

Holly She sucked in a breath. She had always been self-conscious of her nipples. Resembling pencil erasers and surrounded by silver-dollar areolas, they were too big. At least, that's what she'd always thought. The lecherous look in Cowboy's smoking eyes eased her and drove that thought from her lust-filled mind.

When he finally tore his gaze from her chest, he removed her shoes and tugged off her pants. He inhaled sharply.

Was it the thong? Holly didn't normally wear thongs, but this red lace number had been lounging in the back of her underwear drawer for far too long. She'd wanted to feel sexy and desirable this evening.

Able to conquer the world...by wearing crimson butt-floss?

Yeah, it was a sham, but what the heck? She'd worn the thong to accent the freshly trimmed black curls that peeked through the lace.

Clearly cowboy appreciated the gesture. His dark eyes burned.

"Sugar, you are one sexy lady." He didn't remove the thong. Instead, he spread her legs, positioned himself between them, and grasped the triangle of red satin.

When he yanked it toward her navel, she shuddered. The red string rubbed against her clit and moisture dribbled from her, wetting the insides of her thighs. She groaned.

"Yeah, sugar, that's it," he said, continuing to slide the

string through her wet lips. "Saturate this thong and I'll suck the string. Then I'm going to suck you."

Moisture gushed out of her. She knew she was pink and swollen. Her pussy cried out for his tongue, his lips, his fingers, his cock. She wanted it all buried deep inside her.

He buried his face between her legs. "God, you smell good." He tugged on the string again.

Her clit pulsed. When he moved the string over to the side and his fingers grazed her engorged lips, tingles erupted on her skin and her belly fluttered.

"I'm going to suck you now, sugar." His voice had deepened. "I'm going to eat all that sweet cream out of you and you're going to come all over my face."

Sounded good to Holly. She smiled and closed her eyes, but his firm fingers encircled hers.

"No. Watch me." His eyes had darkened to a soft onyx.

He was beautiful. Holly didn't often think of men as beautiful, but this cowboy was.

Hot, sexy, and beautiful.

She pinned her gaze to his as his pink tongue snaked over his full bottom lip—a lip that widened into a sexy smile. He flicked that gorgeous tongue over her clit, and she nearly imploded. Oh, this was going to be one hot night.

His dark hair fell around his golden shoulders and tickled her sensitive inner thighs. She reached forward and sank her fingers into the thick locks. Had she ever felt anything finer? Fine as Persian silk. His lips curled around her clit and he sucked.

Then she did implode. The climax hit her like a lightning bolt, careening into her, humming through her veins and settling between her legs. He licked her relentlessly as the spasms rocked her body. She fisted her hands in his gorgeous hair and pushed his face farther into her wetness.

When the pulsating began to subside, she let her head sink into the soft mattress. He'd climb up to her soon. Hopefully he'd kiss her, sink his tongue into her mouth so she could taste her own sex mingled with his spicy maleness, and then stuff that beautiful cock inside her.

Instead, he grinned, his chin and lips shiny with her wetness. He ripped the thong off her—who needed it anyway?—and clamped his mouth to her folds again.

"Ah..." The soft gasp left her lips in a whisper. She was near climax again.

"Mmm. You're so wet, sugar."

Holly released his hair and slid her hands up her soft tummy to her breasts. She cupped them, squeezed them, plucked at her tight nipples.

When he pushed her thighs forward, exposing even more of her, she twisted her nipples, and icy sparks speared through her. One more lick to her clit—*pow!* She came again, this time with the force of a stampede. Her skin tingled, her heart raced. She moaned. She sighed. She squeezed the soft flesh of her breasts as she came down from the climactic high.

"Mmm," he said, two fingers gently gliding in and out of her heat. "Good, sugar?"

"God. So good."

His fingers slipped from her—oh, the loss!—and he slid forward. He licked her wet curls and circled her navel. He licked her belly, the valley between her breasts. The feel of it was sweet as blueberry syrup.

She sank her hands into his soft hair again. He kissed first one nipple and then the other. He circled the areola and sucked the tight bud between his lips.

"God, I love your nipples."

She shivered, tingled, gasped for air. When he released the nipple, she sighed, but then his lips were on her neck, licking, nipping.

He pulled her legs up over his shoulders and thrust into her.

She widened her eyes. "Condom?"

"Already on," he rasped.

"When?"

"When you...were coming. Ah, God." He pulled out and thrust in again.

Holly dug her heels into his broad shoulders as he fucked her. He fucked her slow. He fucked her fast. He leaned down and kissed her hard nipples. His lips trailed over her cheeks, her neck. Still he fucked her, and damn, it felt so good, so right.

She grabbed his chiseled cheeks and pulled him to her for a deep kiss. Their tongues tangled, dueled, and his soft groans chorused through her like a concerto.

When she broke the kiss to take a breath, he flipped her onto her hands and knees and plunged into her from behind. Ah, the steely hardness of him filling her, the warmth of his strong hands on her hips. He thrust deep inside her, and she slid one hand backward and grasped his sinewy forearm. The flesh was so taut she could feel the lines of his muscles. His fingers found her clit and she shattered again, thrusting backward onto him.

"Yeah, sugar, yeah." He rubbed her to completion. "Come for me. So good."

When her spasms subsided, she leaned forward. He pounded into her once more, holding himself deep inside her.

Each pulse of his cock spiraled against her sensitive tissues.

When he released her, she fell forward and collapsed on the fluffy comforter.

Within a few minutes he lay next to her, pushing moist strands of dark hair out of her eyes. His gaze burned into hers.

"Wow," was all he said.

"Double wow," she agreed.

He kissed the tip of her nose. "Up for an encore?"

She giggled.

When was the last time she had giggled?

"Are you?"

His laugh was husky. "In a few minutes. There is that jacuzzi to consider." He turned onto his back and covered his forehead with his arm.

She'd never made love to a hot stud in a jacuzzi, had never made love in a jacuzzi, period. In fact, she'd never made love to a hot stud, come to think of it, at least not as hot as the cowboy next to her.

Boy, had it been a day. She didn't want to think unpleasant thoughts. She wanted her escape to last a little longer.

She touched his firm lower lip with the pad of her thumb. "I'm up for the jacuzzi, cowboy."

★ ★ ★

Darkness enveloped the room when Holly awoke. Her cowboy was behind her, holding her spoon-style. His large, warm hand cupped her breast. Her sore nipple hardened beneath his palm. A hard thigh was wedged between hers. The soft hair covering his flesh tickled her smooth skin. His breath, slow and steady, blew against her neck and disturbed a few stray hairs.

The night had been amazing—wonderful!—a hedonistic frolic and a total escape. She wouldn't soon forget the encounter in the jacuzzi. How they'd kissed each other until their lips were red and swollen. How he'd sucked on her nipples until they were nearly raw, all the while fussing over how beautiful they were. How she'd ridden him, and the jetting had swished over them as they coupled again, and then again.

A night of wonderful memories to savor was exactly what she had needed.

But now? She sighed as she disentangled herself from cowboy as gently as she could. She didn't want to wake him.

She walked to the window and opened the drapes. The sun peeked over the horizon. Soon dawn would brighten a new day.

She sighed again.

Time to face the music.

CHAPTER THREE

Six months later

Late again.

Holly ran into the classroom, dragging her portfolio behind her. She'd stopped at the art store for more charcoal after work and she'd hit major traffic.

She laughed it off. This was art class at the community college, not a pressing appointment. It was okay to be late. Problem was, she didn't want to be. She wanted to breathe in every bit of knowledge this class and this professor had to offer. She was done taking life for granted. She'd wanted to learn to draw for forty years, and now she was.

She'd always had a flair for sketching—or so others always said. In college she'd taken the well-traveled road and majored in economics and political science and then gone on to law school, which, frankly, had been the three most boring years of her life. She did the time, got the grades, landed the partnership-track job.

Five months ago, she'd thrown it all out with the garbage.

She hated practicing law. She liked to draw. She *loved* to draw. She was good at it. It made her happy. She smiled. What was better than doing what made her happy?

Of course, she had to pay the bills, so she'd hung out a shingle and opened up her own law practice. Writing wills and trusts wasn't exactly a rocket science challenge, but it kept her in food and shelter until she could learn how to make her art pay.

Damn it all if she wasn't happier than she'd ever been.

She hastily took an empty seat and spread out her paper and charcoal. Tonight was model night. Male, if she recalled correctly. Last week they'd sketched a gorgeous blond woman with a body so perfectly proportioned she resembled Barbie.

Well, her legs weren't quite that long.

Drawing the human body fascinated Holly. She'd learned as much about anatomy as she had about technique in this class. She used her knowledge not only in her artwork, but also at the gym, where she was hard at work on another artistic endeavor—reshaping her own physique.

"Good evening."

Holly looked up to see Professor Fleming in front of the class. Professor Fleming was an amazing artist and his praise meant the world to Holly. He liked her work and thought she had potential. Had she started down this path twenty years ago, who knw where she could have gone?

Determined not to berate herself, she looked back up at Professor Fleming.

"Tonight, as you know, we'll be working with a male model. He's waiting outside." He cleared his throat. "I have a special surprise for you all. For the first time, we'll be working with nudes."

Childish chuckles echoed from the back of the room. At forty, Holly was easily the oldest person in this class. Most of the students were straight out of high school.

"Get your jollies out now," Professor Fleming said, "so you don't embarrass our model when he comes in."

Even Holly had to stifle a giggle. Jollies?

When the room quieted, Professor Fleming walked to the door of the classroom. Holly leaned down to grab her bottle of water out of her backpack and then cursed under her breath when she brushed against her charcoal pencils and they tumbled to the floor. She gathered them quickly and decided to leave her water where it was. She could live with a parched throat for an hour. Better that than accidentally spilling water on her art work.

She sighed and looked up just as an emerald silk robe fell from a glorious male body. She glanced at the long perfectly sculpted legs, a back carved of hard muscle, a firm, tight ass. Staring at this for an hour wouldn't be a hardship.

He turned toward the class.

Holly's blood ran cold. Before her was a chest she'd caressed, sinewy arms she'd gripped.

A cock she'd sucked.

Her gaze traveled down the beautiful legs, back up, over the torso dusted with dark hair, the golden shoulders that had tantalized her fingertips to his face of raw male beauty. Cheeks she had cupped, lips she had kissed, sucked on. She wanted to look at his eyes—those eyes that had burned into her soul that night.

That wonderful, terrible, fateful night.

But she couldn't. He might recognize her.

What the hell was a cowboy doing working as a nude model?

Of course, she hadn't asked what he did for a living, because she hadn't wanted to know.

She shook her head to clear her thoughts. He wouldn't remember a one-night stand with a needy older woman anyway. He'd no doubt been glad she was gone when he awoke.

She took a deep breath and raised her gaze to his dark eyes.

He was staring straight at her. Daggers shot from his eyes and speared into her.

He wasn't happy.

Holly's skin prickled. Did he remember her? She couldn't think about that now. She had to draw him.

God, she could draw that body from memory—every line, curve, mass of muscle. She closed her eyes and inhaled, and then opened them and began to sketch. This was class, after all, and she wanted to learn to create art more than anything in the world. She wouldn't let an awkward situation keep her from her goal.

That gorgeous chiseled face... Her pencil stopped moving. He was staring at her again. Damn, those lips were lethal weapons. Her nipples tightened against her bra as she remembered him kissing them, sucking them.

Time to get a grip, Holly. This was art class, and when would she have the chance to draw such a perfect specimen of masculine beauty again?

She sat back and attempted to steady her breathing. *In and out, in and out. Slow down, pulse. He's just a model.*

★ ★ ★

Holly stared at her sketch. It was cowboy, all right. Problem was, he was entwined around a curvy female who bore a distinct resemblance to Holly herself. How had this happened? She'd been in the zone, hadn't thought about what she was doing, and before she knew what was happening, her hands had gone off on their own and drawn cowboy, naked, making love to her.

She couldn't turn this in to Professor Fleming.

Quickly she gathered her papers together and shoved them in her portfolio. If she left now, a few minutes before class was actually over, she could escape before cowboy left the room. She'd draw another sketch—one that wasn't x-rated—at home and bring it to class next week.

Yeah, that would work.

She stood up quickly and quietly and walked out of the room. A sweltering heat swept over her. Cowboy was watching her. She could feel it.

She stopped in the ladies' room and splashed some cold water on her face. It didn't work. She was still hot and bothered, but at least she looked a little better—not pale and wan as when she'd first looked in the mirror. The frigid water had added rosiness to her cheeks. She stood at the counter, grasping the Formica, breathing in and out.

Calm down, Holly. It's over.

After one final deep breath, she hurried to her car and drove the short distance to her downtown loft. Her arms full with her portfolio, briefcase and the small bag of groceries she'd picked up before class, she keyed in the code with her nose and slipped through the door. The elevator was closing so she ran and slid through just in time. She hit the number three with her elbow and collapsed against the elevator wall for the short ride up.

When the door opened, she tightened her grip on all her belongings and headed toward the door to her loft. Dropping the groceries to the floor, she fumbled one-handed in her purse for her key.

Sheesh, it was hot in the hallway. Beads of sweat trickled

from her hairline, down her forehead and into her eyes. She blinked at the sting. Why was it so damn hot?

With an exasperated sigh, she threw down her portfolio and began emptying her purse.

"Need some help, sugar?"

CHAPTER FOUR

That deep, whiskey-smooth voice...

She turned, and there they were—those piercing dark eyes. He looked incredible, almost as delicious as he looked naked. His western shirt was forest green, silky, and unbuttoned at the top. A few black strands of chest hair peeked out. His jeans fit as snugly as she remembered, and he wore scuffed brown leather boots. She could see him on horseback, riding the range, the wind tearing through that gorgeous sable hair.

She looked away and huffed. "What are you, some kind of stalker?"

He shook his head, chuckling. "Can't say I've done anything like this before."

"How'd you get in here?"

"Some doormen can be bribed."

She rolled her eyes. "I don't have a doorman."

He gave a lazy half-smile. "Okay, you got me. Some horny women can be bribed."

Horny women?

"Sheila."

Her man-hungry neighbor had been known to be free with the passcode. Now Holly'd have to call management and get it changed again.

"That her name?"

"Did she have bleached blond hair and a voice hoarse from smoking?"

"That'd be the one." He fingered his stubbled jawline.

Holly tried not to gape.

"Damn her anyway." Holly continued her relentless search for her keys.

Cowboy gently pried the purse from her grasp and pulled out her keys. "This what you're lookin' for?"

She grabbed her purse. "Yes. Thank you, cowboy."

He miraculously picked the right key and fit it into her lock.

"It's Jack," he said. "Jack Sherwood. No more cowboy." He opened the door, picked up her portfolio and bag of groceries and waited for her to walk in.

Her nerves rattled as she entered. He followed her in and set the portfolio and groceries on her kitchen counter.

"Well, thank you for your help," she said. "I can manage now."

"Oh, no," he said. "Not so fast. You haven't told me your name yet, sugar."

"Sugar's fine."

"The hell it is." He walked to the door, shut it, and leaned back against it. "You left me that morning without even waking me to say goodbye. I thought we had a good time. I wanted to see you again. Why'd you pull a stunt like that?"

Holly's heart raced. He'd wanted to see her again? This had to be some kind of sick joke. "It was a one-night stand, cowboy."

"Jack."

She sighed. "Do you understand what a one-night stand is? One night of mind blowing sex? I'm sure you're familiar with the concept."

"That's not what I'm about."

"Well, that's what I was about that particular night," Holly said. "I'm sorry if I upset you. Really I am. I was in a bad place that night and all I wanted was..." She closed her eyes and sighed again.

"You ever going to tell me your name?"

"I think it's better to leave it—" She opened her eyes. "Hey! What the hell are you doing?"

Jack had grabbed her purse from the counter and fished out her wallet. He opened it and pulled out a credit card. "Holly. Holly S. Taylor. What's the S stand for?"

"None of your goddamn business."

"Susan?"

"No."

"Sheila?" He gave a short laugh.

"Hell, no."

He smiled a heart-stopping smile. "Sugar?"

Holly couldn't help but return his grin. "It's Solange, if you must know. It's my mother's name. She's French."

"Very pretty." He replaced the credit card and handed the wallet to her. Her skin tingled when his fingers grazed hers.

"Listen," he said. "You're never going to convince me the sex wasn't amazing that night. I know you felt it."

She shuddered. His voice was like hot silk. "I n-never said it wasn't amazing."

"Truth is, *Holly*, nobody's gotten under my skin like that in...well, ever." He advanced toward her like a wolf stalking its prey.

She backed away, not paying attention to her whereabouts, until she found herself trapped against her own refrigerator. A fairy magnet dug into her back.

"When I saw you sitting in that class today, all fresh and

beautiful, I was both ecstatic and angry at the same time. You know what I mean?"

"N-No."

He placed his palms on the refrigerator, on either side of shoulders, trapping her. His scent drifted around her—cedar wood, spice, and male musk. She could inhale it forever and never tire of it.

"I think you do." He looked above her head for a moment, as if composing himself, and then gazed back into her eyes. "When I woke up that morning and you were gone, I turned that suite inside out searching for something—anything—that would lead me to you."

"I'm sorry—"

"I haven't been able to get you out of my mind." He pressed his lips to her forehead.

She ignited. Blazes trailed over her skin from one little kiss.

"I dream about your nipples, you know that?"

She gulped. Moisture trickled between her legs.

"I dream about suckin' them raw like I did that night. I dream of you suckin' my cock with those sweet lips of yours. Then I dream about fuckin' you hard and fast, and then makin' slow sweet love to you."

Holly writhed under his steady and scalding gaze. Her nipples puckered against her bra. Want—pure, raw want—screamed through her.

His mouth closed over hers. The kiss was gentle at first, tiny licks around the corners of her lips, his tongue like smooth cream. Then he probed with slightly more force and her lips parted. Again, he was gentle, even as he sank into her mouth and kissed her with a slow hunger. It was sweet and sexy at the same time. Nothing like the frenzied passion of their first kiss, but incredible all the same. A soft groan left his throat and vibrated into her mouth, giving her chills.

Holly was vaguely aware of Jack fumbling with the buttons of her blouse and pushing her bra upward. Her ample breasts fell gently against her chest.

His lips left her mouth, and she sucked in a much needed breath. He trailed moist kisses over her cheek, her neck, down her chest, across the swollen flesh of her breast, until he caught a nipple between his teeth.

She couldn't stop her shriek.

He looked up. "Too much?" His word hummed against the wrinkled flesh of her areola.

"God, no, but—"

He took the nipple again and tugged. Lightning flashed to her core and she jerked backward, the magnet digging farther into her flesh.

He let her nipple go with a soft pop. He stood, touching his forehead to hers, his hands cupping her breasts and his fingers gently kneading the tight buds. "Let me back in your bed, Holly." His voice was husky, primal. "*Please.*"

Oh, she wanted to. The thought of another night of unbridled passion with cowboy—no, Jack, what a perfect name for him—sent ripples through her.

But another one-nighter wasn't possible. That wasn't who she was. Jack didn't want her for the long haul, and who could blame him?

She pushed him away and ducked under his arms.

"Sugar?"

"I'm sorry," she said, standing next to the door. "I really need you to go now."

"Holly—"

"Please, Jack."

He walked toward her and smiled. "That's the first time you've called me by my name. I like that."

Why was he so damned sweet? How was she supposed to get rid of him when he made her skin tingle and her heart race?

There was one way.

"I'm forty, you know."

His eyebrows arched. "No, I didn't know. You don't look a day over thirty."

"So you can see the problem."

"What the hell problem are you talking about?"

"Well, clearly I'm a lot older than you are."

He shook his head, his eyes wide. "You really think I give a rat's ass about your age?"

A prickle of defensiveness speared into Holly. "How old are you anyway? Thirty-two? Thirty-three?"

There went the lazy half-smile again. The one that made her heart go pitter-pat. "Twenty-nine, actually."

"Dear God." Holly's body thudded against the wooden door.

"What?"

"What do you mean 'what'?" That's a difference of over ten years!"

He let out a chuckle and then said in an exaggerated drawl, "I done figured that out. Even a cowpoke like me knows how to cipher, ma'am."

"Stop making fun of me."

"Why not, Holly? You're bein' silly."

"Silly? You're young. You're...well, I'll just say it. You're freaking hot. You can have anyone you want."

"Right now, I want you."

"What about tomorrow?"

"Tomorrow, I'm pretty sure I'll still want you. And the next day."

"And after that?"

"Christ, Holly. You want a fuckin' commitment here? It's not going to happen, at least not yet. I'm attracted to you. I'm hot for you. I'm so damned hard right now I think I could cut through diamonds. I'd like to get to know you—inside and outside the bedroom. If that isn't enough for you, well, maybe I *should* go."

Now he was talking sense. As much as she desired him, wanted him, nothing could ever come of it, for reasons she wasn't ready to tell him or anyone else.

"That's right. Go."

"Look—" He gripped her shoulders.

His touch sparked a shiver between her legs.

"I spoke quickly. I don't want to go. If you don't want to go to bed, I can accept that. But can we talk? Have a drink? Or a cup of coffee? We don't have to stay here if you're not comfortable. We can go to a bar or a coffee shop."

Her body was on fire, and she was tempted to spend the evening with this handsome stranger—for that's what he still was, a stranger. However, it couldn't lead to anything good, and she'd just be heartbroken when it ended.

Holly had already experienced enough heartbreak for this lifetime.

"I'm sorry, Jack. Just go. Please."

"Aw, damn, sugar. Why won't you let us get to know each other?"

"Because..." She cleared her throat. His dark beauty

left her breathless. He was a sweetheart and he deserved the best—better than she could give, anyway. She gulped in some courage. "Because I have nothing to offer you, that's why."

"I disagree."

"You don't know me."

"I'd like to change that."

She opened the door and looked at the floor. "I'm sorry."

Tears stung the inside of her eyelids as he walked away toward the elevator.

He didn't look back.

CHAPTER FIVE

He was waiting at her law office the next day.

He looked luscious, of course. He was still wearing jeans and a western shirt. This time the shirt was a creamy beige that accented his golden skin tone. Could he be any more tempting?

"Mr. Sherwood's been waiting for a while, Holly," Cindy, the receptionist, said. "Said he had an appointment."

Holly let out a harsh breath. Reprimanding Cindy would do no good. The young woman took phone calls and manned the lobby, and each tenant contributed to her salary. But each tenant who rented an office here kept his own calendar. Executive suites, the offices were called, and many sole proprietors found them an economical way do business while keeping the professional air of a downtown building. The situation usually worked just fine.

"Is everything okay, Holly?" Cindy asked. "It's not like you to miss an appointment."

I don't miss an appointment...when I have one. Holly smiled at the receptionist. "Just running late is all." Now, what to do with Jack? He'd already been waiting and to keep him any longer would look bad to Cindy. "Come with me, Mr. Sherwood."

She opened the door to her office, gestured him in, and closed the door. "Don't you have a home to go to?"

"Yup." He took a seat in one of the chairs in front of her

desk. He looked completely comfortable and at ease. And absolutely edible.

Damn him.

"Then why aren't you there?"

"I have a legal problem."

"How'd you find me?"

"A little bird." He chuckled. "With a raspy voice and smoke on her breath."

Holly rolled her eyes. "Sheila. One day I'm going to revert to my teenage years and kick that woman's ass. I could take her, you know."

Jack's smile lit up the room. "Aw, leave her alone. Poor thing's going to be on oxygen in ten years anyway."

"That's her own doing."

"True enough, but don't blame her. I was persistent."

"Of course I blame her. She should keep my private information private."

"Sugar, your business name and address are hardly private. I would have found you eventually. Sheila just sped up the process a little by telling me you were an attorney. It was easy enough to find you after that." He leaned toward her and whispered. "I could've Googled you and found you myself."

Holly moved away from him. Being too close to him kept her from thinking straight. She sat down behind her desk, inhaled, and looked right at him, determined not to be mesmerized by his dark gaze. "What is it that you want, Jack?"

"Besides you in my bed?"

A rush of heat crept over Holly's skin. She cleared her throat. "Yes, besides that."

"I told you. I have a legal problem."

"Which is?"

"I need a document drawn up, giving me sole custody of my son."

An anvil landed in Holly's stomach. He had a son? "You have a son?"

"Sugar, you look like someone just told you pigs could fly. Surely this can't be that surprising."

"Well, I just—"

"If you'd had that drink with me last night, so we could get to know each other, I would've told you all about Sam."

"And his mother?"

"Was a mistake I made seven years ago. No, I take that back. She wasn't a mistake, or I wouldn't have Sam. She came to me a year later. He was only a few months old. Said she couldn't take care of him, that he was mine. So I took him."

Holly stomach was churning. Jack was not who she thought he was. He wasn't a player, wasn't just after sex. "Did it occur to you to have a paternity test?"

"Yep. I had it. He's mine."

"Whatever happened to your...his mother?"

"Never heard another word from her."

"Is your name on the birth certificate?"

"Yes."

"Then there shouldn't be any problem. The mother clearly abandoned him. If you haven't heard from her in six years, why are you worried about it now?"

"It's something I've put off long enough. I need to tie up some loose ends."

"Good enough. I have to tell you though, this really isn't my area. If you had Googled me, you'd have found that I'm an estate planning lawyer. I write wills and trusts. I don't dabble in family law."

"I want you to handle it."

"I'm not qualified. I have a rolodex full of great family attorneys who will be more than happy to help you."

"I want you."

She let out a sigh. "You're not hearing me, Jack."

"Correction, sugar. You're not hearing *me*." He stood, walked around the desk, and turned her chair to face him. One long finger gently nudged her chin upward. "I'll take the referral to a qualified attorney. I want this done right. But I'm still going to be here every morning until you agree to have coffee with me. Just coffee. No alcohol. No dinner. No kisses, no sex. Just one hour, Holly. That's all I'm asking. One hour to get to know a little about me, and I'll get to know a little about you. If you still want to say goodbye after that, I'll walk away."

"But I'm too old for you."

"Bullshit." He glided his fingers over her jawline to cup her cheek. With the calloused pad of his thumb, he lightly stroked her bottom lip.

She closed her eyes. His touch felt so wonderful, so perfect.

Would it really hurt to have coffee with the guy? They had no future, but heck, some caffeine and a heavy dose of cowboy drawl sounded pretty good right about now.

Oh, she'd regret it. Spending time with him would make it all that much harder to say goodbye. God knew, though, she'd been through worse.

"All right." She placed her hand over his, still holding her cheek. It was firm, warm, and masculine and made her heart flutter.

Okay, that was a mistake. She brushed his hand away from her face and dropped her own to her side and stood. "Let's go."

They ended up at the coffee shop across the street, a little mom and pop shop called Mocha Dreams that had, so far, stood up to Starbucks. Jack bought Holly a vanilla latte and he had black coffee.

"I'm a purist," he said.

She couldn't help but smile.

"So," he said, handing her the latte and pulling out a chair for her at one of the little round tables. "Tell me about Holly Taylor."

"There's a loaded question." Holly tried to sound nonchalant. There was both nothing and everything to tell. Her life hadn't been that exciting. "I'm from here originally. Where are you from?"

His grin split his face. "Texas."

Of course. The drawl, the persistence, the raw male beauty, his size. Everything about Jack Sherwood was *big*.

"Okay, I'm dying to ask. Why were you modeling nude last night?"

His laugh filled the room. "I was doing a favor for a friend."

"For who?"

"Mark Fleming, the teacher."

"You know Professor Fleming?"

"He's my godfather."

This just kept getting better and better. Holly shook her head and took a sip of latte.

"So you were out late last night and up with the birds this morning. Where's your boy?"

"Sam's with my mom for the week, having some grandma time. Mom knew I was helping Mark out, knew I'd be out late. I'm modeling for all his classes this week, not just yours. Some are during the day."

"What do you do otherwise?"

"I run a small ranch about an hour from here, so I'm used to getting up early."

Holly shook her head again. "You're not anything like I expected."

"What'd you expect?"

"I don't know. Kind of a cad, you know? A guy who'd bed a woman without knowing her."

"Seems I recall the whole thing was your idea, sugar. Who was I to say no?"

"You're right." Holly couldn't deny it. That night *had* been her idea. She'd used him, really. It hadn't been a nice thing to do. "I'm sorry."

He grinned. "You hear me complainin'?"

"Well, no, but—"

"Sugar, the only complaint I have is that you left without saying goodbye. I wanted to see you again."

"Like I said, Jack, I was in a bad place then. I needed something. Someone. You were there, and you gave me a nice memory. It meant more than you know."

"I don't want to be a memory, Holly. I want to see you."

"I'm too old for you."

"That's the dumbest thing I've ever heard."

"It's not dumb. You're just starting out in life, and I'm—"

"For Christ's sake, Holly, you're forty. You're not dead!" He looked around and lowered his voice. "I got a bigger bang out of being with you than I've ever had with a woman. I haven't been able to get you out of my mind. Yeah, the sex was great. It was earth moving. I won't lie to you. I want more of it. But I want to get to know you, too."

"Now you know me. I'm Holly. I'm forty. Single, never

been married. I'm a lawyer who wants to draw. Enough said."

"Why don't you want me?"

Holly's mouth dropped open and she stared at his chiseled face. "Are you serious?"

"Well, something's keepin' you from seein' me again."

"It's... It's the age thing, cowboy." She swallowed. "That's all."

"Not good enough, sugar." He stood and tossed his empty coffee cup in the nearby wastebasket. "We're going out tonight."

"Jack, I have class."

"Mark doesn't have a class tonight."

"It's not Mark's...Professor Fleming's class. It's a different class. Conceptual drawing."

"Skip it."

"No. Drawing is my passion. I don't want to skip it."

"I'll make it worth your while."

"Damn it, Jack. Why are you so determined?"

"I do whatever I can to get what I want, sugar. Right now, you're it."

Holly sighed. "Tomorrow night?"

"Don't want to wait. But tomorrow will be, if that's what it takes. The day after, I pick up Sam from my mom's, and my time'll be more limited." He grinned. "In fact, tomorrow's perfect."

"Perfect?" What did he have in mind? And why did tomorrow sound like it wouldn't work? "Oh!" She clapped her hand to her mouth. "Tomorrow's no good. I have to go to Professor Fleming's—"

"Exhibit," Jack finished for her, still smiling. "I figured you'd like that idea, so I'll be takin' you. We'll have dinner first. Deal?"

Warm tingles spiraled through Holly. He understood how much the exhibit meant to her. Maybe, just maybe...

She sighed.

No.

This was only temporary. Once Jack found out the truth about her, he wouldn't want her anymore.

CHAPTER SIX

"How am I supposed to walk through Professor Fleming's exhibit after that meal you just fed me?" Holly patted her full tummy. "You're going to have to roll me out of here."

Jack's husky chuckle was too low to resonate over the din of the restaurant, but Holly felt its vibration. Very sexy. Then again, everything he did was sexy.

"You do like a good steak, don't you, sugar?"

"Yes, I do."

His smile was pure sin. "So many women these days won't eat red meat. Heck, they won't eat anything but rabbit food."

"Well, I enjoy eating," Holly said, "and life is too short not to do the things we enjoy."

"True enough," Jack agreed.

He had no idea how true. The man hadn't even hit thirty yet. The whisper of a chill skittered up Holly's neck. She hated thinking about his age. Thinking about his age led to the myriad reasons they could never be together long term. That saddened her, truly. She liked this man more with every minute she spent in his company. He was so much more than a hot cowboy. He was a father, a son, a rancher. Her lips curved. A nude model.

She had to end it tonight. The more time she devoted to him, the harder the heartbreak would be when it ended.

And it *would* end. That was inevitable.

"So you ready?" Jack said.

Holly nodded and rose. "Yeah, let's go. Thanks so much

for the dinner."

"My pleasure." He stood and helped her with her light sweater. "The gallery's only a block away. Nice night for a walk."

She nodded again. "I'd like that."

"You okay, sugar? You sound a little down all of a sudden."

Just thinking about turning you loose tonight.

She sighed. "I'm fine, Jack. Just a little tired. But I don't want to miss this exhibit. I'm a huge fan of Professor Fleming's work. I hope this exhibit will be his big break."

"He's hoping so, too." He took her hand and guided her around the tables and out the door of the restaurant.

He continued to hold her hand as they walked. The spring night was balmy, and downtown Denver was hopping. Every woman who passed them seemed to be checking Jack out, and Holly couldn't help but wonder what they thought of her, the older woman, on the arm of the hot young cowboy. Her skin prickled with conspicuousness. They didn't talk during the short walk, and Holly breathed a sigh of relief when they entered the small gallery.

A hostess greeted them with glasses of wine and a tray of *hors d'oeuvres*, which Holly declined. She was so full from dinner she might never eat again.

"There's Mark," Jack said, gesturing. "Want to go say hi?"

Holly shook her head. "I'm sure he's busy."

"Not too busy for his favorite godson." Jack pulled Holly along behind him as he made a beeline for Professor Fleming.

"Jack, good of you to come," Professor Fleming said as they approached. "Meet my agent, Mary Rivers."

A small blond woman held out her hand.

Jack shook it, and then said, "This is Holly Taylor."

"A pleasure, Ms. Taylor," Professor Fleming said. "You look familiar. Have we met?"

Holly cleared her throat. "I'm in your perceptual drawing class at the community college."

"Ah, yes, that's it." He reddened just a bit, but Holly noticed. "Then you were there when Jack—"

"Yeah, she was, but that's not how we met, so get your mind out of the gutter." Jack exchanged a smile with the older man.

Holly's cheeks warmed. Get his mind out of the gutter? If he knew how they'd actually met, he wouldn't think the whole nude model thing was that bad.

She stifled a giggle. "I'm really excited about this exhibit, Professor."

"Please, call me Mark, and I hope you enjoy it," he said. "I know Jack'll take good care of you."

"Count on it, Mark." Jack excused himself and Holly and led her to the first wall of oil paintings.

Holly didn't enjoy abstracts much, so she was glad Mark had only a few in his exhibit. She much preferred landscapes and portraits. She drank in the colors, the textures, examining each painting closely and then from farther away.

"Wow," Jack said beside her, his warm breath caressing her neck.

"What?"

"You're looking at each one like it's unique."

"Each one is unique, silly."

"That's not what I meant. Heck, I don't know what I meant. It's just...beautiful, the way you sink into the art, like you're becoming one with it."

"I kind of am, I guess. I love art. I always have. I should

have learned to create way before now, but"—she sighed—"life gets in the way sometimes. Decisions get made for the wrong reasons."

Jack said no more, and Holly went on to the next painting. It was a little boy on a chestnut horse. Clad in jeans and cowboy boots, he looked to be about five or six years old. Mark had captured his youthful beauty with tiny strokes of the brush. The child's dark hair and eyes gazed outward, as if he were looking through Holly.

"Gorgeous," she said under her breath.

"You like that one?" Jack said.

"Yes, it's wonderful. The horse and the child almost seem like one being, and the child's innocence is depicted so beautifully. I can't believe Mark is only now showing this stuff."

"Oh, I think it's kind of like you said. Decisions get made. He didn't decide to get serious about his own work until later in his life."

"That's sad. I hope this exhibit is successful. In fact, I think I'd like to buy this painting."

"I don't think that particular one's for sale, sugar." Jack handed her the program. "It's not listed."

Holly leafed through the pamphlet. He was right. "Shoot. Well, I'd like to support my professor. I'll have to find another, I guess."

Holly chose a painting of an older woman gardening. It didn't move her quite as much as the little boy on the horse, but it was beautiful nonetheless, and the color scheme would look great in her loft. She and Jack said goodnight to Mark and took the downtown shuttle back to Holly's loft.

Jack smiled as he entered the passcode. They took the elevator up, and she fished her keys out of her purse and handed them to Jack.

Why had she handed the keys to Jack?

It had been an unconscious move on her part. Weird.

He unlocked the door and followed her in. He set the painting on the floor and smiled at her.

That gorgeous, sexy, heart-stopping smile.

She was a goner now. She knew exactly what he was after, and she wanted it, too.

Was one more night with him too much to ask? Another night of mind-numbing sex that she could remember when it was all over?

"Jack—"

He pulled her to his body, gripped her cheeks with his warm hands, and lowered his mouth to hers.

His full lips were smooth and firm, laced with the lusty spiciness of the Petite Sirah they had drunk at the gallery. Slowly they slid over hers, kissing, caressing, urging, until Holly had no choice but to open to him. The kiss was slow at first, thoughtful, unlike their previous encounters, but its depth evoked powerful emotion from her head to her toes. His lips were numbing, drugging, and they carried her to a place where she felt, for a moment, a happy ending might exist for them. She allowed the illusion to saturate her mind and gave herself freely to his leisurely passion, meeting his gentle tongue with her own, exploring his sweet mouth with a soft fervor.

It was a beautiful kiss, unlike anything she'd experienced. One hand remained firmly on her cheek, and his thumb caressed her as though she were made of fine porcelain. His other hand trailed down her neck and made her shiver as he gently massaged her nape. Such wonderful, talented hands.

The kiss continued. He didn't touch her breasts, didn't

pull her closer into his arousal. She fought her own desire to grind into him, to unbutton his shirt and trail her fingers over his sculpted chest, his copper nipples. Instead she reached upward and tangled her fingers in his silky hair.

Holly lost track of time. Had it been only minutes? Or maybe half an hour? Still his lips held her in thrall, and the kiss chorused like a symphony through her veins. Perfect.

The perfect kiss.

Her nipples puckered against her bra and moisture trickled between her legs. Still he kissed her lips and nothing more.

When he finally pulled his mouth from hers, he looked down at her, his eyes burning, and smiled.

"Holly," was all he said.

She wanted to tell him what that kiss had meant to her, that she would cherish it always. She parted her lips, but no words emerged.

"Sugar, that was the best kiss of my life."

"Oh, Jack, me too."

His fingers still caressing her cheek, he said, "I'm glad to hear that. Glad this isn't just one-sided."

Holly widened her eyes. "How could you think that?"

"You don't seem to want me like I want you."

Holly touched his lips, swollen and wet from the kiss. This man was so beautiful "Wanting you isn't the issue, Jack. It never was. How could any woman not want you?"

He kissed the tips of her fingers and then gripped her shoulders and pulled her against his body. His arousal poked into her belly.

"Feel that? That's me wanting you, Holly. That's me dyin' to make love to you."

"I—"

"Please. Please let me take you to bed tonight."

Holly closed her eyes and buried her head in his hard shoulder. He didn't know, but she had already made her decision. She would take him to bed.

Tomorrow she'd tell him goodbye.

CHAPTER SEVEN

She had the world's sexiest nipples. Jack couldn't get enough of Holly's breasts—their full, round shape, their soft flesh, and especially those amazing rosy nipples that fit so well between his lips. They were smooth as satin beneath his fingers and tongue, and they tasted like sweet cream. He'd never known a woman's nipples to have a flavor, but Holly's did.

He couldn't wait to get inside her hot body that gripped his cock like no other. He hadn't had sex since the night they were together. Sure, he'd had the chance, but he hadn't wanted to. Strange, but Holly had gotten under his skin that night, and when he'd stood before her art class, naked as the day he was born, both joy and anger had seized him—joy that he'd found her and anger that she hadn't wanted him past that one night.

She was hiding something. That much was clear. At this particular moment, though, he didn't much care what it was. He burned for her, and he was going to have her.

She writhed under him as he licked her nipples, sucked them, bit them. She liked her nipples bitten hard, his Holly, and he was happy to oblige. He trailed his fingers over her soft belly and entwined them through her dark thatch of curls. Nearly black, they were a few shades darker than her long mahogany hair. Why that turned him on, he couldn't say, but he itched to inhale their muskiness, to sink his tongue into the moist folds they hid. He sifted through the curls to find her swollen clit and he rubbed it as he continued to tug on her nipple.

"God, Jack," she moaned. "Please."

He released the tight bud and smiled. "What, sugar?"

"It feels so good. Put your fingers in me, Jack. Please."

Never one to deny a lady, he inserted two fingers into her hot, wet channel. She clamped around him like a vise, and he nearly lost his load right there. She was so tight. He couldn't wait to sink his cock into her.

He glided in and out of her, enjoying the tight suction of her walls around his fingers. Twisting his hands, he massaged her G-spot and she arched upward. His forearm tensed as he added a third finger, stretching her willing flesh for his hard cock.

He couldn't take much more, but first he needed to taste her. He unclamped his lips from her gorgeous nipple and let his tongue travel over the round flesh of her breast, down her silky belly, and through the pretty, dark curls.

He lapped at her folds, the honey and spice a pleasure to savor, as he continued to finger fuck her. She writhed and moaned, sweet symphony to his ears, and he closed his lips around her clit and sucked.

"Yes, Jack, yes!" she rasped, her voice low with desire.

Her walls spasmed, milking his fingers with their sweet contractions. When the convulsions slowed, he sucked her clit and made her come again, just for the sheer pleasure of hearing her moan his name.

"Jack."

Not cowboy. Jack. How sweet the sound from her pink lips.

"Fuck me now, Jack," she said, "please."

Removing his fingers from her took effort, but knowing he'd replace them with his cock made it worthwhile. With haste, he found his jeans crumpled on the floor and withdrew a condom from the pocket. In seconds, he sheathed himself and returned to Holly's bed.

He lay next to her and touched his lips to hers, slowly tracing them with his tongue. He loved to kiss a woman after he'd gone down on her. He had no idea why, but shoving his tongue coated with female musk into her mouth never failed to get him going. Of course, he was horny already, but when Holly opened for his kiss and he fed her a taste of her own juices, a spike of intense heat hit him low in the gut.

He caressed her smooth skin, trailing his fingers along her back to the soft curve of her bottom. She had a great ass, just plump enough. He squeezed a firm globe of flesh, and a rumble escaped low in his throat. He had to have her. Now.

Still cupping her backside, he glided on top of her and slid himself snugly between her welcoming thighs. He thrust inside, and the breathy sigh from Holly warmed his neck and made his skin prickle. He buried himself to the hilt and stayed immobile for a moment, letting himself sink into her tightness. His body was ablaze—hard, hot, and filled with lust—yet he needed this closeness, this chance to consume her completely, before he began pumping into her.

Holly had other ideas. She rocked her hips against his, and tiny tremors shook his cock. He withdrew slowly and plunged back into her depths. Ah, how her tight suction gripped him, moved him. He thrust into her again and once more. He wanted to give her more, but he was so close. His body ached for release. The slender length of her legs cushioned his pistoning hips, and he groaned when her walls clenched around his rock-hard shaft. She was coming, thank God. He let himself go and the vibrations began in his balls as they tightened against his flesh and then traveled through his cock in tiny jerks.

"Holly, sugar," he gasped and spilled into her warmth.

She clutched his ass, pushing him farther into her as he came with violent jolt after jolt of heavenly pleasure so intense it almost hurt.

When his body finally relaxed, she caressed his back, murmuring unintelligible words against his neck. He kissed her sweat-dampened forehead and rolled to his side. His cock, still hard, slid out of her.

"Jack," she said.

"Hmm?" He flung his arm over his forehead. His breathing was unsteady.

"That was amazing."

He couldn't help but smile. Hell, yeah, it had been amazing. He pulled the soiled condom from his penis and disposed of it in the wastebasket next to her nightstand. He turned to her, her beautiful face glowing with the sheen of perspiration.

"It was goddamned fucking amazing, sugar. The best I've had in years. Maybe ever."

Her smile illuminated her beauty. Had he reached her? Would she give him a chance now?

"Come here," he said.

She scooted into his arms.

He kissed the top of her head and pulled her close. "Sleep now. You're going to need it."

★ ★ ★

Holly couldn't sleep. Jack's hard body snuggled up to her felt so good. Why couldn't her life have turned out differently?

Why couldn't he have been born ten years earlier and

already had all the kids he wanted?

Face it, Holly. No matter how you slice it, this wasn't meant to be.

She disentangled herself from his muscular limbs and padded out to the kitchen for a glass of water. If only he weren't so sexy, so handsome. But his looks and charisma weren't what had her so shaken. It was him. Jack. Sure, he had a gorgeous face, an amazing body—but that was superficial. What she loved about him was his kindness, his persistence, his nurturing personality.

Holly's glass clattered to the bottom of the stainless steel sink. Luckily it didn't break, and she hoped the noise didn't wake Jack.

Shit. Had she just thought the word "loved" about Jack?

God, Holly, you so can't go there.

Heart-stopping sex does not equal love.

Hands shaking, she retrieved her glass, filled it with cold water, gulped it down, and splashed the still-running water on her face. She reached for her dishtowel and rubbed the wetness from her skin.

She'd spent two nights with the man. Had two dates with him, if you counted the coffee date yesterday morning. She couldn't possibly be in love.

Her pulse raced. She was more than a little freaked out. He was too young for her, that was for sure, and there were definitely other reasons he wouldn't want her. Damn—how could she love him? What a perfect setup for heartbreak and that she did not need.

With a huff, she strode to the extra bedroom that housed her computer. She sat down and typed "older woman/younger man" into the search engine bar.

Over a million hits!

Apparently she wasn't the only woman who had the hots for a younger man.

Curiosity got the better of her, and she began clicking. Lots of information surfaced and she skimmed it, but when she stumbled into a chatroom called "The Cougar Club" she had to take a closer look. Maybe these ladies would understand her dilemma. Surely one of them might have a similar issue.

She created an account under the name HollyGolightly— not original but she couldn't think of anything else at midnight—and logged in. Music jingled, indicating a post.

ILoveCubs: *Hi, Holly!*

GoodtimeCharlene: *Evening, Holly.*

MrsRobinson: *Hey there, Holly! Welcome!*

Should she lurk? Only these three were in the chatroom besides her. She'd be very conspicuous if she lurked.

She'd log out. This had been a mistake. She was no cougar. Jack wasn't a cub. It wasn't going to work out anyway, due to circumstances way more important than their respective ages. Her mouse was poised over the logout link when the jingle sounded again.

ILoveCubs: *Welcome to The Cougar Club.*
Is there anything we can help you with
tonight, Holly?

Just click, Holly, just click.

As seconds passed, she knew she wouldn't leave the chatroom, but she didn't chat, either.

MrsRobinson: *Or just feel free to lurk if you're more comfortable with that. Charlene was just telling us about breaking up with her latest.*

GoodtimeCharlene: *Yeah, it didn't work out this time. My first foray into cougardom. But I enjoyed his stamina :).*

Should she? Why not?

> **HollyGolightly:** *If you don't mind my asking, why didn't it work out?*

GoodtimeCharlene: *Not at all. He's only thirty-five, and he wasn't ready to give up the dream of a white picket fence and a houseful of rugrats.*

Holly's heart sank. Jack was six years younger than Charlene's "cub."

ILoveCubs: *And you're not willing to talk about that?*

GoodtimeCharlene: *Hell, no. Been there, done that. I'm done being the soccer mom. My children are in college.*

MrsRobinson: *If he loves you, he'll be willing to compromise.*

GoodtimeCharlene: *What compromise is there? He wants a child of his own. I already have children of my own, and my child-bearing years are rapidly coming to an end. I just don't want to do it all again.*

ILoveCubs: *Understandable.*

MrsRobinson: *Never say never. There's always a compromise available.*

ILoveCubs: *I'm not sure there is, Megan. Children can be an issue that ends a cougar/cub relationship. I've seen it happen too many times.*

MrsRobinson: *Katelyn, I don't want to sound all Pollyanna, but if they love each other, they can work it out.*

Holly made a mental note—ILoveCubs was Katelyn and MrsRobinson was Megan. She wondered how old they were.

GoodtimeCharlene: *I have to side with Katelyn on this one, Megan. I just don't think there's a future with Bob. Yeah, I love him, but he's not willing to give up his dream of being a parent, and I have to respect that. If I were twenty years younger, it would be my dream too.*

A lead ball dropped to Holly's stomach. It all came down to children for Charlene and Bob. That part of Charlene's life was over, but it hadn't yet begun for Bob. Children were the issue. And of course they were. They'd been Holly's dream, too.

HollyGolightly: *If you don't mind my asking, how old are you, Charlene?*

GoodtimeCharlene: *Don't mind at all. I'm forty-seven. How old are you?*

HollyGolightly: *Forty.*

MrsRobinson: *I'm fifty.*

ILoveCubs: *Me too. How old is your cub, Holly?*

Her cub? Jack was her cub? The beginning of a smile curved her lips.

HollyGolightly: *He's twenty-nine.*

MrsRobinson: *Nice!*

ILoveCubs: *Have you been together long?*

HollyGolightly: *No. And it's not going to work out anyway. There are issues.*

MrsRobinson: *There are always issues, hon. But we can help, right, ladies?*

GoodtimeCharlene: *We can try. That's what we're here for.*

HollyGolightly: *Are you ready to say goodbye to Bob, Charlene?*

GoodtimeCharlene: *No, to be honest. But I love him enough to let him go. If he lets go of his own dream to be with me, he may resent me for it, and I don't want that.*

Holly nodded at the computer screen. Charlene, whoever she was, spoke the truth. Resentment had no place in a relationship. Did she love Jack enough to let him go?

She nodded again. What a mess! She was in love with Jack.

ILoveCubs: *Do you have anything you want to tell us, Holly? You're safe here.*

Safe? Safe in a computer chatroom talking to faceless women? Heck, she didn't even know if they were women. They could be perverted old men who got off on talking about young studs.

Somehow she knew this chatroom was legitimate. She felt it, and she felt safe. And she did need to talk to someone.

She started to type, but the soft thump of footsteps behind her interrupted her thoughts. Quickly she clicked on the logout link.

"Sugar?"

She turned to face Jack, who looked tousled and sexy and

way too good for the middle of the night.

Her heart sped up at the sight.

"What're you doin' up? You okay?"

She stood to face him. "I'm sorry if I woke you."

"You didn't. I just rolled over and you weren't there. Brought back memories of that morning after, till I remembered I was at your place. Pretty hard for you to run out on me."

Holly smiled and pushed back a lock of dark hair that had fallen over his eye.

It hit her again, like an arrow between her eyes. She was in love with this young cowboy, and it was time to let him go.

She'd do that in the morning. For the rest of the night, she could lie in his arms and make love to him. For just a few more hours, she could play Pollyanna like Megan and pretend everything would work out.

Tomorrow would be soon enough to end it.

CHAPTER EIGHT

"What?"

The forkful of scrambled eggs on its way to Holly's mouth dropped back onto her plate.

Jack smiled at her from across the kitchen table. "I said I want you to spend the weekend with me."

"You're kidding."

"Nope. I want to see more of you, and I want you to meet Sam."

"I don't think I'm ready to—"

"No excuses, Holly. Don't tell me you didn't feel something special last night. We made love four times. Four, sugar. I'm twenty-nine, not seventeen. I haven't been able to make love four times in a row for nearly a decade."

"Maybe you just haven't had any in a while?" Holly's voice hedged.

"You're right about that. Not since that night with you."

Her fork crashed onto her plate next to the discarded serving of eggs. He hadn't had sex since her? Well, she hadn't either, but he was a guy—an incredibly sexy and desirable guy. Surely women fell all over him, especially with all that nude modeling.

How was she supposed to end this? To love him enough to let him go, like Charlene said, seemed impossible.

"Look, Jack—"

"Sorry." He stood and placed his empty plate in her sink.

"Not taking no for an answer this time. We have something special here, Holly. I want to get to know you, and I want you to get to know me and my son." He hesitated for a moment and a troubled line creased his forehead. "You do like kids, don't you?"

"Yes, of course I like kids, but—"

He leaned down and brushed his lips over hers. "Good. I'll pick you up at your office tomorrow at five. Have your bag packed."

"Jack, really—"

"Got to run, sugar." He thumbed her cheek and kissed her again. "I'm pickin' up Sam this morning at my mom's, and then I have some stuff to do around the ranch today. I'll see you tomorrow evening."

In a flash, he was gone, leaving Holly with her mouth hanging open.

★ ★ ★

Her bag was packed. She'd told herself she wasn't going, that she couldn't put Jack through this, but in the end, she had gathered her sundries and clothing and packed them in her burgundy overnight bag. It now sat by the door to her office.

He was late. It was nearing five thirty, and all her office mates and Cindy had left early for the long Labor Day weekend. Jack hadn't said anything about the long weekend, but Holly had packed for three nights just in case.

She frowned. If he stood her up...

A soft sigh left her throat. If he stood her up, it would be for the best. Though her heart cried at the thought, at least it would spare her having to end it after the weekend.

After she'd fallen that much deeper in love with him.

Five thirty went by, and then five forty-five. Holly stood from her desk, ready to take her packed bag home, when Jack rushed in.

"Thank God you're still here," he said, panting.

"What happened?"

"Just ran up here from where I parked a block away. I was afraid you'd have left already."

"I was just about to."

He grinned. "I'm glad I got here in time. Sorry to be runnin' so late."

"Is everything okay?"

"Fine. Just had to run a quick errand, and Friday night traffic was bad."

"Oh."

"Sam's anxious to meet you."

"He is?"

"Sure is. Believe it or not, I don't bring lots of ladies home, and he loves company. He says he wants to show you his horse. Sound good?"

Holly absently rubbed her bottom. "I've never been on a horse in my life."

Jack let out a laugh. "We'll remedy that this weekend." He walked behind her desk and embraced her. "Damn, I've missed you."

She let out a nervous giggle. "You just saw me yesterday."

His lopsided grin stole her breath. "I still missed you, sugar. How about a kiss?"

Before she could reply, his lips crushed to hers. This wasn't the gentle kiss of two nights ago. This was a desperate kiss, a possessive kiss, as though he'd been hungry for the taste of her for days, weeks. He thrust his tongue into her mouth with fierce determination and devoured her.

She loved every second of it.

She kissed him back with equal fervor. God, she'd missed him, too. She hadn't realized how much.

Moisture trickled between her legs. One kiss, and she was ready to be thoroughly fucked.

He broke from her mouth, panting. "I need you, sugar. Are we alone?"

"Yeah." Her voice was low and raspy. "Everyone else left for the day."

"Good." He lifted her skirt, moved her panties aside, and thrust his fingers into her. "Already so wet for me. Do you have any idea what you do to me, sugar?"

"Maybe a little." Her breath came in a puff.

"God, you've got to know." He turned her and bent her over her desk. Her stapler bit into her midsection, but she didn't care. She heard the zing of his zipper and the rip of a condom packet.

"You ready for me?" His low voice was music to her ears.

"Yes. Please."

He thrust into her in one smooth stroke. He'd barely plunged in the second time when her walls clenched, sending icy spasms from her womb to every cell in her body.

"Jack, yes!" Ripples pulsed through her.

"Yeah, sugar, come for me. Just like that." He thrust into her again and then once more, burying his cock in her as he cried out his own release.

The weight of his body pushed her farther onto the stapler and the hardness of her wooden desk. He pressed wet kisses to her neck, making her shudder as her orgasm continued to roll through her. She panted against her day planner, and beads of sweat trickled across her cheeks and dropped onto the open book.

"Holly, I wish..." He rose, leaving her feeling an acute loss when his body heat and weight left her. With a tender touch, he replaced her skirt and panties.

She unbent her body, turned, and faced him. "You wish what?"

"Nothing." He smiled, disposed of the condom, pulled his pants around his luscious narrow hips, zipped them, and buckled his belt. "Come on. It's a forty-five minute drive to my place from here. Luisa's keeping dinner for us."

"Luisa?" Holly pictured a sultry Hispanic woman as she smoothed her underwear and skirt.

"She keeps house for me and watches Sam while I work," Jack said. "Her husband is my hired hand around the ranch."

Husband. Whew. Holly relaxed a little.

"Do they live on your ranch?"

"Yeah. There's a small house adjacent to the main house. They live there."

"That's handy."

"Works for all of us. At least it will till they decide to have their own family. Then I'll need to find different help."

"Oh." Everywhere around her, it seemed children and family were the focus. Always a reminder of why this relationship with Jack wouldn't work long term.

But why think of that now? She could enjoy the weekend with him and meet his son. She just wouldn't get attached—to his son or to his home, that was. She was already attached to him, and heartbreak was just around the corner.

She forced a smile. "Ready?"

His grin lit his raw male beauty. "You bet."

★ ★ ★

Holly laughed as they rode through the gate to Jack's ranch. The sign above it said *Rancho Notso Grande*.

"Nice name."

He chuckled. "Sam came up with it."

"Did he really?"

"Yeah. Luisa teaches him a little Spanish now and then. Her husband, Carlos, doesn't speak much English, and Jack wanted to talk to him. Last year he decided our little operation needed a name, and that's what he came up with."

"He sounds smart."

"I'm sure I'm a bit biased"—Jack winked at her—"but I think he's the most brilliant six-year-old on the planet."

Holly couldn't help but smile. Jack loved his son. He was a doting daddy, as he should be. If only...

He pulled his red pickup to a stop in front of a sprawling ranch house.

"Wow," Holly said under her breath.

"It looks bigger from the outside," Jack said. "It's actually pretty cozy."

Warmth crept to her cheeks. "I didn't think you heard that. It looks gorgeous to me."

"I hope you like it." He exited the truck and in seconds opened the passenger door for her. All that and a gentleman, too.

Oh, this would be difficult.

He grabbed her overnight bag out of the back and led her up the driveway and into the house.

"Daddy!" A small boy ran into Jack's arms.

"Hey, buddy." Jack pulled the child into a bear hug and kissed the top of his head. "I want you to meet Miss Holly. She's the friend I told you about."

The boy turned to Holly and she melted. He was Jack in miniature, only his ebony eyelashes were even longer than his father's, if that was possible. He had the same dark eyes and sable hair, and an adorable elfin face that promised handsomeness in the future.

"Welcome to Rancho Notso Grande, Miss Holly." He held out his little hand.

Holly melted into a puddle. *What a cutie.* "I'm so pleased to meet you, Sam," she said, taking his small hand in hers, "and you can call me Holly. I hear you named your dad's ranch."

"Yup. Sure did."

"It's a fine name." She smiled and was overjoyed when he smiled back, showcasing a missing front tooth. *Adorable.*

"Did you already eat, Sam?" Jack asked.

"Yeah. I ate with Luisa and Carlos. Sorry, Daddy, I was hungry."

"That's okay. But Miss Holly and I are starved, so we're going to go to the kitchen and eat our supper. Where's Luisa?"

"She's in the kitchen."

"Okay. You run along and play for a little while. It'll be bedtime soon."

"Okay."

"What a good natured little thing," Holly said to Jack, as he led her to the kitchen.

"Yeah, he's a good kid."

As Holly had originally feared, Luisa was indeed a Latin beauty with black hair and eyes, red lips, a sumptuous figure.

She stood at the sink rinsing dishes.

Husband, Holly reminded herself. *She's no threat.*

Not that it mattered anyway.

Jack made the necessary introductions and a few minutes later Sam ran in.

Luisa caught him in a hug. "Come on, *mijo.* Let's get you ready for your bath." She excused herself and left the kitchen with Sam.

She'd left them a Mexican feast—cheese enchiladas, *refritos,* and *carnitas,* which Holly had never eaten before. It was stewed pork served with guacamole, sour cream and *pico de gallo.* It was delicious and very spicy.

Her nose was running after the first few bites.

Jack laughed and handed her a box of tissues from the counter. "Sorry, sugar. Luisa only knows how to cook hot, hotter, and hottest."

"No problem," Holly said and meant it. "I love spicy food, really. This is just a little spicier than I'm used to. But it's wonderful, and it's homemade. I don't get to eat homemade food very often."

"You don't cook?"

"I love to cook. But what's the point of cooking for one? Frozen entrees are cheap and easy."

"When's the last time you cooked?"

"Heavens, I don't know."

"Do you have any specialties?"

"Well, yeah, actually." Her cheeks warmed. "I told you my mom's French. I make a mean *boeuf bourguignon.*"

"Sounds delicious. What is it?"

"It's beef stewed in red wine, and it's divine. In fact"—an idea came to her—"why don't you give Luisa the night off tomorrow, and I'll make it for you and Sam? You'll love it, I promise. I'll have to start it in the morning. It cooks for several hours and the whole house will smell great."

"What do you need? I'll have Luisa go to the market."

"A nice lean cut of beef, about two pounds. And a dry red wine. Some pearl onions and mushrooms. Thyme and bay leaves. Especially the thyme. That should do it. Oh, and flour, unless you already have that. It's a staple in most kitchens."

"Now, sugar, flour I have. I make a mean flapjack myself."

"Okay then." She shot him a grin. "I'll expect your flapjacks for breakfast, and I'll make you a great dinner."

"Sounds like a deal." Jack sipped his glass of Chardonnay.

Holly, who normally only drank red wine, had to admit the oaky white worked well with the spicy Mexican fare.

Luisa whisked into the kitchen. "Sam's ready to say goodnight."

"I'll be right up," Jack said, rising. "Excuse me for a few minutes, Holly."

"No problem. Take all the time you need." She turned to Luisa. "Thank you so much for the delicious dinner. I can't remember when I've enjoyed a meal more."

"You're most welcome, *señorita*."

"Please, call me Holly. I'd love to get your recipes if you don't mind."

Luisa laughed and Holly was again stunned by her fresh beauty. "I never write them down, but I can show you. Tomorrow?"

"I told Jack I'd cook for Sam and him tomorrow. Maybe the next day?"

"*Si*, Carlos likes a good Mexican feast on Sundays. I'll be happy to show you then." She sat down in the chair Jack had vacated. "Tell me, Holly, how long have you known Jack?"

"Not long. Why?"

"Because he hasn't brought a lady home for a while. I don't keep track, but it's been more than a year, close to two at this point."

"Oh?" Holly's heart jumped as a sizzle of happiness raced along her nerve endings.

"He was very excited to have you come. He kept me busy all day making sure the house was clean and neat for you. I've never seen him like that."

"You didn't need to go to any trouble for me."

"I'm glad to do it. Carlos and I, we want Jack to be happy. He's a good man."

"Luisa, Jack and I..." Holly hedged. "We haven't been together very long. It's too soon for any type of real commitment between us."

Luisa smiled. "I understand. It's just good to see him interested in someone."

Holly returned Luisa's smile. She couldn't help but like the younger woman. Beneath her dark beauty shone kindness and what Holly sensed was true caring for Jack and his son.

"Do you have children, Luisa?"

"No. Carlos and I have tried for years, but it hasn't happened for us yet. I have Sam. Carlos and I love him like he's our own. And we have lots of nieces and nephews who we dote on. Most of Carlos's family is still in Mexico, but I have seven brothers, and they all have kids." Luisa's black eyes filmed over—only a bit, but Holly noticed.

And she understood.

She reached across the table and patted Luisa's hand. "It may happen yet, Luisa. You're young."

"Yes, I am only twenty-seven. I pray every night for a baby of my own. Until it happens, I take care of Sam for Jack."

"How long have you been taking care of Sam?"

"Since he came." Luisa's eyes crinkled as she smiled. "Carlos and I have been on the ranch since we got married. I was only nineteen at the time. Carlos didn't speak much English, so I came with him to speak to Jack about working here on the ranch. My mother works for his mother, and she sent us over here."

"Does his mother live nearby?"

"*Si*, on a neighboring ranch. His father passed away last year."

"I'm sorry."

"He was very ill with cancer. It was for the best."

The C-word. Chills crept up Holly's spine. Would she ever be able to say it out loud? There was so much she didn't know about Jack, and so much she wanted to learn, but wouldn't be able to.

"Sam's all tucked in." Jack's voice boomed as he entered the kitchen.

"I'll get home, then," Luisa said, rising. "It was great talking to you, Holly."

"You too," Holly said and meant it. "I'm looking forward to our cooking lesson on Sunday."

"I thought you said you could cook," Jack said to Holly, his gorgeous full lips curved into that lazy half-smile she adored.

"I can. American, French, a little Japanese even, but not Mexican. I want to learn."

"Luisa's the best, then. I'll stay out of your way on Sunday."

They laughed as Luisa left.

"I took your bag upstairs for you," Jack said, pulling Holly to her feet.

"I suppose you have a guest room?"

"I do. But I was hoping you'd stay with me."

Her tummy fluttered. "You know I'd love to, but Sam..."

"I'm a grown man, sugar. Sam doesn't have any say about who I sleep with."

"Are you sure?"

"Well, I could put you up in the guestroom, but I'd be sneakin' in there with you. And if Sam woke up in the middle of the night lookin' for me and I wasn't there, that'd sure be more traumatic for him then finding a hot woman in my bed."

Holly couldn't help but laugh. Why was he so damned wonderful?

"What do you want to do tonight? We can watch a movie. I have a great DVD collection."

"How about a walk? I'd love to see more of your ranch."

"I do like the sound of that, sugar, but I sent Luisa home. I can't leave Sam."

"Oh." The warmth of embarrassment coated Holly's cheeks. "I'm sorry. I'm not used to being around kids. I don't know what I was thinking."

"It's okay. I hope you'll get used to Sam, though. I want you to get to know him. He's a wonderful kid."

"I know that already." She cupped his cheek tenderly, let her fingers scrape over the rugged stubble of his night beard. "And he has a great dad."

Was that a blush on his neck and cheeks? He was so handsome, and his humility made him more adorable.

"I promise you a great tour of the place tomorrow, with Sam and me as guides." He covered her hand, still on his cheek, with his own.

Its warmth radiated through Holly's skin all the way to her core.

"Tonight, though, I can give you a bird's eye view of the Big Dipper from my deck, if you'd like. You can see stars out here that you just can't see in the city, sugar. It's amazing."

"I'd love that." She leaned upward and brushed her lips gently over his.

He deepened the kiss, but only for a moment. "We can make love under the stars, Holly." His low voice hummed against her lips.

"How is it that you do this, Jack?"

"Do what?"

"Make me want you so much? It's like I'm not myself anymore. I can't see. I can't hear. I can't even breathe."

His lips moved against hers in a smile and he nipped her chin. "I'm so glad this isn't all one-sided. You're so beautiful. I can't get enough of looking at you. And right now, I want to look at you under the Big Dipper."

CHAPTER NINE

Jack's redwood deck wrapped around the back and both sides of the ranch house. They sat together on an old-fashioned porch swing holding hands, not saying much, until the sun set and the stars shone in the black night sky. Holly's breath caught at the beauty of it all. Jack had been right. The country sky held secrets she'd never seen. The Big Dipper was vibrant in its luminescence, and lesser stars she hadn't known existed twinkled all around it.

Once she'd breathed in her fill of the night sky's radiance, Jack undressed her slowly, kissing each new inch of skin as he exposed it. When they were both naked, he grabbed the blanket hanging over the back of the porch swing, took her hand, and led her to a secluded spot on the soft grass.

The sounds of the evening shrouded them—crickets chirping, a delicate breeze rustling through the aspen grove that surrounded Jack's house, and the soft groans rumbling from Jack into her as he made love to her slowly, sweetly, and gently underneath the stars.

Later he led her to his bedroom and made love to her again.

★ ★ ★

"It's easy, Holly, you just stand on the near side and get on."

"Near side?" Holly eyed Sam's eager face, and then turned to the creamy white animal that was already saddled. "You mean the one I'm nearest to?"

"He means the left side, sugar," Jack said. "You need to speak in non-cowboy language for Holly, Sam."

"Sorry, Daddy. But I can't believe she never rode a horse before!"

"She lives in the city, pal. Not everyone lives on a ranch like we do."

"Well, everyone should."

Jack laughed. "Can't argue with you there." Then to Holly, "Just put your left foot in the stirrup, and hold onto the withers."

"Jack"—Holly rolled her eyes—"what the hell is a wither?"

"Non-cowboy lingo, Daddy," Sam reminded him.

Jack's lazy smile lit up his face. "It isn't that easy, is it, pal? The withers, sugar, with an 's.' It's the highest part of the back at the base of the neck."

He patted the horse's withers, or so Holly assumed.

"Ladybelle here is gentle, and she'll take good care of you."

"I hope so. I have to say, I'm a bit nervous."

"The horse'll sense your fear, Holly," Sam said. "Right, Daddy?"

"Sam's right, sugar. You need to take control."

"Right. Take control of an animal that outweighs me by four times."

Jack eyed her and she warmed under his gaze. "I'd say about eight or nine times, sugar. But that'd probably make you more nervous."

Holly's tummy lurched. Eight or nine times? "Thanks for that, Jack."

"Aw, Holly," Sam said, "Ladybelle's our most gentlest horse here. I've been ridin' her since I was knee high to a grasshopper."

Holly shook her head. Sam wasn't much more than knee high to a grasshopper now. "Okay, here goes." She grasped the "withers" and lifted her left leg into the stirrup. Quite a difference from the only stirrups she'd encountered in the last year—those at the gynecologist's office. Her skin chilled for a split second until she wiped the negative image from her mind. Today was for her and Jack and Sam. She'd worry about the rest tomorrow.

Make that Monday.

Tuesday at the latest.

"Okay, sugar, just push up with your left leg and swing your other leg over the back of Ladybelle there, onto the saddle."

"But be careful you don't kick her flank," Sam warned, "or you'll knock the wind out of her."

"Flank?"

"Right between the ribs and the hip," Jack said. "Just be careful. You won't kick her."

"From your mouth to God's ears," Holly mumbled. Just what she needed, an angry horse who couldn't breathe while she was completely helpless, one leg lodged in a stirrup. She inhaled sharply and swung her leg over Ladybelle's body.

Her bottom hit the hard saddle with a plunk.

"There you go," Jack said. "Now gather the reins and slide your other foot into the stirrup. Are you comfortable? Are the stirrups the right length? I can adjust them for you."

"How the heck should I know? They feel okay."

Jack gazed down at her feet. "Yeah, they look okay. You should be able to slide into them simply by lifting your feet a few inches. Now you wait while Sam and I get on our mounts, and we'll start out."

"Uh, Jack?"

"Yeah?"

"She's not going to...take off or anything, is she?"

He laughed. "No, sugar. Just sit tight. We'll be with you in a minute."

Jack helped Sam onto a spotted gray horse and then mounted his sleek brown horse with smooth grace. Damn, the man was beautiful.

"Okay, sugar. We're going to start with a slow walk. Just squeeze your calves together, and Ladybelle'll know what to do."

"Don't I just say 'giddyup' or something?"

Sam burst into giggles.

"No, Holly," Jack said. "Just squeeze your calves. Don't kick, or she'll get numb."

"I'd never kick any animal, Jack Sherwood."

"I know you wouldn't. I'm just sayin' don't squeeze too hard. Sam, come on." Jack's horse walked.

Holly stared at Jack's finely shaped calves and tried to see exactly what he was doing. Underneath his jeans, those muscular legs were no doubt taut and sinewy with their squeezing movements. Unfortunately, she couldn't see through the fabric, so she had to guess how much tension to put in her own legs.

Sam followed his father, and Holly took a deep breath. It's now or never, she said to herself, and squeezed her calves together.

To her astonishment, Ladybelle walked. The horse followed Jack and Sam. Holly's bottom bounced a little in the saddle. Jack and Sam seemed to be sitting comfortably. What was she doing wrong?

"Pull back the reins now," Jack said. "We need to stop and check the girth."

"My girth is just fine, thank you."

"Oh, sugar, your girth is lovely. But we're checking Ladybelle's girth."

Holly pulled on the reins and Ladybelle jerked to a stop.

"A little lighter pull next time," Jack said. "Now watch me." Jack slid his fingers beneath the band that went under the horse and held the saddle in place.

At least that's what it looked like it was doing. Holly didn't have a clue.

"If you can get more than two fingers under the girth, you need to tighten it."

Her hands shaking, Holly replicated Jack's actions. Barely one finger fit between the girth and the horse. "Good to go, I guess," she said.

"Excellent. Let's try a slow walk again. You know what to do."

"Jack, I—" She stopped. How exactly could she say her ass was bumping in the saddle? Not very sexy. "Never mind."

"How're you doing, sugar? You ready to trot?"

"I'm not sure."

"Sure she is, Dad." Little Sam sped forward.

"He's quite the horseman," Holly said.

"Sam would rather ride than just about anything else. Now, for the trot. While we're walking, squeeze her side with your legs again, and she'll move to a faster pace. Just a warning, though. It's going to get bumpy."

Bumpy? Bumpier than it was already? She was going

to need a sitz bath for sure. *Epsom salts, here I come.* She squeezed her calves, and Ladybelle started to trot. At least Holly assumed it was a trot. The way her ass was plunking up and down didn't bear any resemblance at all to what Jack and Sam were doing ahead of her.

Jack slowed down and soon rode beside her. "Uncomfortable?"

"Just a touch."

"Try to move with her movement. I know it's hard at first."

"Hard doesn't even begin to describe it."

"I'll massage you later." His dark eyes gleamed.

While a massage from his master hands sounded like heaven on earth, Holly wasn't anxious for him to see her bruised behind. "No thanks."

He laughed. "Don't underestimate the therapeutic value of a good butt massage. Try to post to the movements. Post up and down in the saddle in time to the beats of the trot."

"Right."

"Sometimes it helps to say 'up, down, up, down.'"

"You're kidding, right?"

"Nope. That's how I learned."

"But you weren't forty years old."

"True enough. I was four. Just like Sam was."

"I'm afraid I'm old and set in my ways. I love horses. I really do. They're noble and beautiful animals but I'm not sure I was meant to ride one." *Up, down, up, down.*

It wasn't working.

"Anyone can ride a horse, Holly. We all start out the way you're starting out. It's completely normal."

"Come on, Jack. You look like you were born on a horse."

"Hell, no. I did my share of fallin' the first day. You're doin' way better than I did."

"You were four."

He chuckled. "I suppose it helped that I had no fear. Four-year-olds don't, as a rule. But as an adult learnin', you have sense enough not to spook the horse. So you're ahead of me."

"I don't particularly feel ahead of anyone at the moment."

Plunk, plunk. The bones in her butt ached. Weren't butts supposed to have lots of cushy insulation?

Jack whistled to Sam. "Turn around, pal. I think Holly's had enough for this mornin'."

"Oh, I hate to cut his ride short."

"No worries. I can take him out again this afternoon if he wants. Or he can ride by himself, as long as he stays close to the house."

"Are you sure?"

"Sure, I'm sure. We'll have loads more opportunities to bring you out here."

Holly's insides squeezed together. There wouldn't be loads more opportunities. This was probably the only time she'd visit Jack's ranch and the only time she'd ride a horse.

"Besides," he continued, "you need to get back to check on that great meal you put in the oven before we left, right?" He winked.

"Not really. It bakes for several hours. I don't need to do anything."

"I was tryin' to give you an easy way out, sugar. I know your posterior's hurtin'."

Holly sighed. It was, at that. The massage Jack had mentioned was sounding pretty darn good.

★ ★ ★

She was sitting on a hemorrhoid donut pillow.

Her humiliation was now complete.

Thank God she hadn't fallen off Ladybelle. That would have been the ultimate embarrassment. Right. As if the donut weren't enough.

Luisa had brought her the pillow after lunch. She'd said it had been her mother's.

Of course, Holly was old enough to be Luisa's mother—her young mother, but mother nonetheless.

She sighed and brought another forkful of *boeuf bourguignon* to her mouth. At least her dinner had come off without a hitch. Jack hadn't stopped raving about it. Even Sam was gobbling it up, and Luisa had told her the little boy could be picky.

Watching him with Jack was a joy. Their easy banter, the closeness between them, made Holly wonder about Jack's birth mother. Who was she? Holly had given Jack the names of a few good family lawyers in Denver. She shuddered to think what might happen if the woman showed up and demanded rights to her son, or worse, sued for custody. That would kill Jack.

Hate for the woman who'd borne Sam bristled at Holly's neck. That dumb woman didn't know how lucky she was. How could she have abandoned such a sweet little boy? What Holly wouldn't give to...

No. Such thoughts had no place.

She'd ask Jack about the situation once Sam was in bed tonight. That's the least she could do since a long term relationship between them wasn't possible. She'd see that he got a good family law attorney and make sure all paperwork regarding Sam was in order.

After dinner, they sat on the deck while Sam ran around the yard with Jack's dogs, Lacy and Max, two happy and panting Golden Retrievers.

They didn't say much, just held hands and watched the horseplay.

After half an hour, Luisa came out to collect Sam for bed.

"Go ahead, partner," Jack said. "I'll be up to read you a story once you've had your bath."

"Can Holly read me my story tonight?"

"Sam, Holly's our guest."

Holly warmed, pleased that Sam felt close enough to her to ask her. "I'd be happy to read to him, Jack. I don't mind."

Jack's smile heated her. God, she'd miss him—his raw male beauty, his amazing sexual prowess. But mostly she'd miss his gentleness, his devotion to his son, and his big heart.

"If you're sure you don't mind."

"Not at all."

"Okay." He gave her a chaste kiss on the cheek. "After you're done with Sam's story, I have a special surprise for you."

"Oh, you do?" She arched her eyebrows, hoping she could pull off a seductive look.

"Get your mind out of the gutter, sugar. Though I have plans for that kind of surprise as well. This is something tangible. And you're going to love it."

CHAPTER TEN

"It's me, sugar."

Holly inhaled, her skin tingling, as she gazed upon the beautiful painting of the boy on the horse she'd wanted to buy at Professor Fleming's exhibit. She and Jack stood in his small den, which was next to the kitchen. The canvas sat upright on a camel-colored leather sofa.

"That's why it wasn't for sale. It belongs to me. I loaned it to Mark for the showing. He painted it when I was six, just Sam's age. I want you to have it."

She gasped as tiny tingles raced across her flesh. He was giving it to her? Something so precious? As much as she adored the painting, she couldn't take it. It wouldn't be fair, not when she wouldn't be sticking around.

"Jack, I can't accept it. It's something special from your godfather to you."

"But I want you to have it. I saw the way you looked at it. You have an appreciation for it that I can never share. I mean, it means a lot to me because it's from Mark, but you understand the art. What he was tryin' to convey. To me it's just a pretty painting."

"How can you say that? Okay, maybe you're not that into art, but he painted it out of love for you. Can't you see it? It's all right there on the canvas. This is more to you than a work of art, Jack. Much more."

"I understand that. Honestly, I do. And I want to give it to you."

"But that means..."

"It means you mean a lot to me, too."

Holly's heart dropped to her tummy. God, she loved this man. She was so head over heels in love she couldn't tell up from down. But as much as she loved him and as much as she adored the painting, she couldn't accept it. To do so would be to perpetuate a lie, a lie she'd already been perpetuating far longer than she should have. She knew better. She and Jack had no future, and it was time to tell him why.

A tear trickled down her cheek. She'd lose him today.

Forever.

His long finger wiped the tear from her face. "What's wrong?"

"It's a beautiful painting, Jack. And even more beautiful is the sentiment behind it and the fact that you want me to have it."

"You're beautiful, Holly. The most beautiful woman I know, inside and out."

But he didn't know her inside. That was the problem.

She took a deep breath, opened her mouth, and...

"Jack, tell me about Sam's mother."

Fucking coward.

He smiled. "Does this mean you accept my gift?"

No. "It means I'll think about it."

"Okay, good enough. For now. What do you want to know?"

"Let's start with her name."

"Isabel Watkins. She was a cocktail waitress in a small ranching town on the eastern plains. She was nineteen and needy, I was twenty-two and horny. That about sums it up."

"Was she pretty?"

"Pretty enough. Not as pretty as you."

"Jack..."

"Yeah, she was pretty. Had dark eyes and hair like me, which explains why Sam looks like he does."

"Sam looks just like you. He's the spitting image of you in the painting."

"Yeah, a little."

"A lot. You're both beautiful."

"Shucks, ma'am," he drawled, "I ain't beautiful."

She swatted him in the arm. "Of course you are, and you know it. You've surprised me at every turn, Jack. I never would have imagined that my hot one-night stand would turn out to be such a fine man."

"I don't go out lookin' for one nighters, Holly. I want you to know that. Sam came from a one-nighter, but I was younger then. Not as discriminating."

She grinned. "Just a young and horny cowboy, huh?"

"Something like that."

"You're more than just a horny cowboy. More than just a nude model. Though I can certainly see why the modeling appeals to you. You get to show off that magnificent body of yours."

"Sugar, I don't do it to show off my body."

"I was just teasing, Jack."

"I know. But the nude modeling appeals to me for another reason. The money. It pays two hundred dollars an hour."

Holly widened her eyes. "Mark pays you that much?"

"The college does. Big universities pay even more. It's a drop in the bucket compared to what it would cost to hire a real model to take his clothes off."

"Is it weird going naked in front of your godfather?"

"Nah. He's an artist, and I'm just a model. He offered me the job because he knew I'd jump at the chance to make the extra income. My ranch is a small operation. Don't get me wrong. I do fine, but Sam and I aren't rollin' in it by any means. The extra bit helps."

"Ah, I see." She gave him what she hoped was an impish grin. "So your body had nothing to do with it?"

"Well..." His face reddened.

God, he was so adorable.

"Students do need a...good physique to learn to draw the muscle groups and all. But you're a student. You know that already."

"So you're admitting you have a good physique?" she teased.

He pulled her into his arms and nuzzled her neck. "I'll admit it when you admit you have a luscious physique. In fact, maybe you should model nude."

She pushed him away, laughing. "When pigs fly, Jack Sherwood. No one wants to look at a forty-year-old woman naked."

"I do." He moved forward and pressed his lips to hers in a gentle kiss. At the same time, he began to slowly unbutton her white blouse. "You have no idea what I went through that night I saw you in Mark's class. Mind over matter, sugar. I had to work to keep from sproutin' a giant hard-on in front of twenty-five college kids." He stroked the flesh above her breasts.

She shuddered and then giggled. "Might have made for some interesting drawings for Mark to grade."

He let out a chuckle. "My godfather and I aren't *that* close. I have no desire for him to see me with a woody."

She giggled again. Who was this strange woman? She felt

like she was eighteen again, in love for the first time.

"But when I saw you sittin' in that classroom, all I could think about were those gorgeous nipples of yours, those cherry lips around my cock." He grinned. "I had to close my eyes and think of England."

"Ha-ha," she said, trying to keep it light.

But light it wasn't, as he unsnapped the front clasp of her bra and let her breasts fall free. He pinched one nipple and then the other, and heat pooled between her legs.

"I can't get enough of you, sugar. Each time I make love to you, after I come, I'm hard again in almost no time flat. The more I have you, the more I want you." He leaned down and nuzzled her breast. His evening stubble was heaven scraping against her hard nipple. "I've never felt this way before."

"Oh, Jack..." Neither had she, but she couldn't say so. Not when it would be over in two days.

"You don't have to return my sentiment, Holly. I understand it might be too soon for you. But I want you to know how I'm feelin'. I'm not just after a piece of ass."

"I know that, Jack."

"Good." He took her nipple between his lips and tugged gently.

"Jack?"

"Hmm?"

"Should we...go to the bedroom?"

He let go of her nipple with a soft pop and gave her a lascivious grin. "I'd kind of like to try out my leather couch."

He moved the painting to his mahogany desk near the back of the den and then grabbed Holly and took her lips in a deep kiss. The forceful demand of his mouth against hers, the moist heat of his tongue, left her shaking, yearning for more.

Once again her passion overrode her caution, and she found herself wanting—needing—his body inside hers.

Stop him, her inner voice warned. *Stop him and tell him the truth. You're not being fair to him. To Sam. Even to yourself.*

Her longing for him silenced her conscience and she responded, kissing him with a raw, devouring fury that overwhelmed all rational thought.

Jack, inside me. I need Jack inside me.

Her lips still glued to his, her tongue deep inside his mouth, she took charge and ripped open the snaps of his sage green western shirt, the pop of each snap resonating in her ears and bringing her closer to her goal.

Jack, naked. Her lips around his cock. His fingers embedded in her. Their bodies joined in ecstasy.

She pushed the soft fabric from his shoulders. How glorious his golden muscles felt under her fingertips. When the shirt had pooled in a heap on the carpet, she went to work on his pants. Still their lips remained joined.

He kissed her with a fervor, a frenzy, a mind-numbing surety, and she returned it with equal zeal.

When his jeans were open, she pushed them and his boxers to the floor and urged him toward the couch. She ripped her mouth from his, whimpering at the loss, and pushed him down on the leather sofa. Still clothed, though her breasts hung free, she lowered herself to her knees and took that beautiful cock between her lips.

She wrapped her mouth around him tight and sucked.

"Ah, God," he groaned.

She let him go and teased him with little flicks of her tongue around the swollen head. He grabbed her head with his strong hands and tried to force her back onto him. She resisted at first, but then couldn't help herself. She took him deep, deep into her throat. She loved this cock. She loved sucking it. Loved the salty male flavor of him.

Most of all, she loved the man attached to it.

She pulled back, licked the underside, and nuzzled his balls. She inhaled his musky rawness. She could never get enough of his scent, his touch, his kisses.

His groans fueled her passion. She took him deep into her throat again, and he pulsed against the roof of her mouth.

He pushed her head off him. "Not yet," he said. "God, you drive me crazy, but I don't want to come yet."

"Please, Jack," she said, wanting this more than she thought possible. "Please. I want you to come in my mouth."

"Holly..."

"Please. I want it so bad I can taste it already."

"Damn." He fisted his big hands in her hair and guided her back down on his cock.

The tiny spasms began in the back of her throat and spread along his whole length. She sucked in time with him, milking him, and letting his come trickle over her tongue. It tasted salty, bitter, but she didn't care. To her, it was sweeter than fresh cream.

When his shaft relaxed, she released him and smiled. His eyes were closed and a sheen of sweat coated his handsome face. A drop meandered through his night beard, and she caught it with the tip of her finger. He opened his eyes and smiled at her.

"Wow."

"Yeah, wow. Why didn't you want me to do that?"

"I wanted to come inside you."

"I hope you weren't disappointed."

"Are you kiddin'? It was amazing. I just didn't want to leave you hangin'."

"Who says I'll be left hanging? I happen to know you've got more to give, cowboy."

"Well, yeah, ma'am." He tweaked a nipple. "I'm pretty sure I can pony up to the challenge."

"I thought you might be able to." She slid down his body and removed his boots, his socks, and his jeans which were still around his ankles.

"We've got one problem here, though," he said.

"What's that?"

"You're wearing too many clothes."

"Hmm." She grasped his hands, pulled him into a stand, and sat down on the couch. His cock, at perfect mouth range, was already growing again. She grabbed the cheeks of his taut ass and kneaded them. He was so damned gorgeous. She cleared her throat. "I don't really see the problem, Jack."

He leaned down and gave her another soul-searing kiss. She sighed into his mouth as he slid her blouse and bra over her shoulders.

He stopped the kiss, nibbled on her lower lip, and trailed little pecks to her ear. "The problem, sugar, is that I want you naked. Naked, under me, wailing my name as I pound my hard cock into you." He cupped her mound through her jeans. "Does that work for you?"

"God, yes." Her breath came in rapid puffs as he fingered her swollen clit through the thick fabric. The textures, the wetness between her legs, everything worked to send her over the edge. She was near climax already.

"Jack..."

He continued his ministrations, now pressing little love

bites to her sensitive neck. "Hmm?"

"God, Jack, I'm... I'm..."

She burst into flames.

"Coming, Jack. I'm fucking coming... Ah, God!"

The spasms ripped through her, her skin chilling, her pulse racing. When they finally slowed, she was panting against his gorgeous hair.

"See?" She took a shallow breath. "I knew you wouldn't... leave me hanging."

"Not in this lifetime." He grinned. "And we're not even close to finished yet." In record time, he freed her of her shoes, jeans, and panties and sat down on the couch with her in his lap. He grabbed her breasts and squeezed them.

"I've said this before, sugar, but your nipples are like candy." He sucked on one and then the other.

Icy tingles danced across her flesh. His mouth was so sexy. His lips suckling her was a delicious sight. His cock pulsed under her. He was ready again.

Though it took great effort, she pulled her nipple from his mouth and slid downward. She could gaze at his sculpted chest forever. She lowered her mouth and kissed his chest, swirling her tongue first over one coppery nipple and then the other. She licked him and caressed him with her tongue.

"Nice, sugar."

"You're gorgeous, Jack. "

He groaned, lifted her hips, and set her on his cock. She inched downward, taking every sweet centimeter of him.

She sighed. So good. "Thought...you wanted me under you."

"This'll do for now."

"Yes. It. Will."

She sat up and sank down farther, until he was balls deep, and she swore part of his cock was reaching her soul.

She lifted her hips and took him even deeper. She started slowly but soon quickened her pace and rode him with an impassioned vengeance, her boobs jiggling, her body throbbing. He grabbed a nipple in his mouth as she rode him. He nipped her, sucked her, and she cried out when her orgasm exploded inside her.

Still she rode, her walls tightening, taking him hard and fast as her convulsions continued.

"You're so tight, sugar." His voice came in breathless pants. "I'm going to come now. Take all of me." He grabbed her hips and slammed her down upon his cock.

Her sensitive walls felt every pulse of his climax. She caressed his chest, placing her palm over his heart as it beat in time with his release.

She lifted her gaze and met his dark eyes. They burned with passion.

He smiled.

She smiled back.

No words were necessary.

But as she laid her cheek against his chest, his heartbeat thrumming against her ear, her conscience resurfaced, and her eyes misted.

The end was near.

CHAPTER ELEVEN

"What are we going to do today, Daddy?"

Jack tossed the skillet with a flick of his wrist, and the pancake he was frying flipped over perfectly.

"Can you do that with an omelet?" Holly asked, smiling.

"Never tried it."

"My daddy can do anything." Sam beamed proudly, his missing front tooth making his smile all the more loveable.

"I'm sure he can." Holly turned to wink at Jack.

He winked back. "Haven't had too many complaints about my skills."

"You didn't answer my question," Sam said. "What are we going to do today?"

"Well, it's Sunday. How about we get our chores done early and spend the day relaxing with Holly. I owe her a walk around the ranch."

"A walk? Boring!"

"You can stay here with Luisa if a walk doesn't appeal to you. Holly and I can take Lacy and Max with us. They'll love it."

"No, I wanna go," Sam said.

"Good," Holly said. "We'd love your company." She meant it. The little boy had wormed his way into her heart in but a day.

"Yep, we sure would, pal." Jack slid the pancake onto Sam's plate. "You want another, sugar?"

"Are you kidding? I'm stuffed. I shudder to think how much you're going to have to feed Sam when he hits his teens." She laughed. "You'll go broke."

"Just like my mom and dad did." Jack let out a chuckle. "Teenage boys are bottomless pits. Don't I know it." He turned to Sam, who was busily buttering his flapjack. "You stay here with Holly for a few minutes. I need to make a phone call in the office."

"Okay, Daddy."

Holly eyed the boy as he slathered syrup over the pancake and then dived in. He was a beautiful child. If only...

"What kind of things do you like to do, Sam? Other than ride horses and help your dad."

"Lots of things," he said through a mouthful. "Play games with Luisa and Carlos. Sometimes I get to spend the night at their house. Or at my grandma's. That's fun. She makes really good cookies. Chocolate chip are my favorite."

"They're my favorite too." Holly smiled.

"Plus, there's some kids my age who live close to my grandma, and she invites them over when I'm there. Derek and Kathleen. They're twins."

"Oh?"

"Yeah. They're six too, and it's fun to play with other kids. There aren't any who live around here."

"I'm sorry about that. Do you get lonely, Sam?"

"Sometimes. When Daddy's workin' all day and Luisa's busy. One day, I hope I'll have a little brother. I really want a little brother. I've wanted one forever. Daddy says maybe someday. I've been waitin' a long time."

Holly's throat constricted and her tummy sank to her bowels. Icy fingers crept along her spine. Sam wanted a little brother.

Luisa hurried into the kitchen waving a dust rag. "Off, you two. It's time for me to clean up in here."

Holly stared at Luisa and then said in a robotic tone, "Please, let me do it."

"Nonsense, it's what I'm paid for. You go have a fun day with Jack and Sam."

A fun day with Jack and Sam. Right. The air in the kitchen seemed thick, suffocating.

Little brother? Oh, God.

"Luisa? I need a favor."

Luisa turned from the sink. "What do you need? I'll help if I can."

"Sam? Can you run along and play for a little while? I need to talk to Luisa."

"Sure thing. See you later." He ambled off, whistling a lively tune.

"What is it?" Luisa asked, concern etched along her brow. "Is something wrong?"

"I'm afraid so. I need to leave. I don't have a car. Jack drove me."

"What's wrong? Is it an emergency?"

"No, no. Nothing like that." *The only emergency is that I need to get out of here.* Her breath caught in her chest. *Breathe, Holly. Breathe.*

"How can I get a ride home? Will a cab come out here?"

"Carlos can drive you home. He gets Sundays off."

"God. Thank you. I'll owe you both big time. Where's Jack?"

"He's in his office. Then he said something about checking on a few things in the main barn."

"Will he be gone long, do you think?"

"I don't know. You can run out and tell him what's going on."

"No!" Holly adjusted her voice quickly. "I'm sorry. I didn't mean to sound so upset." But upset she was. "I need to get home right away. How quickly can Carlos get here?"

"In a couple minutes. Please, Holly, can you tell me what's wrong? Jack will be worried."

"It's nothing to worry about. Just something came up that I need to take care of."

"What do you want me to tell Jack?"

"Just that. I'll... I'll call him later. Tell him not to worry."

"Okay. If you say so."

Holly raced to the bedroom while Luisa picked up the kitchen phone, presumably to call Carlos.

Within fifteen minutes, she was packed and in Carlos's truck, driving toward downtown Denver.

The only problem was, she'd left her heart at Jack's ranch.

★ ★ ★

Jack didn't call her. Hell, she didn't blame him, the way she'd run off like a freaking coward. Minutes turned into hours as she lay on her bed, holding her pillow to her face, inhaling Jack's scent. She'd never wash that pillow case. How long would the aroma last? It would slowly dwindle away, and she'd be left with nothing.

Why had she fallen in love with him? A man so young, so vibrant, with a beautiful little son who deserved so much more than she could ever give either of them.

Now she had no one to turn to.

It served her right for leading Jack on far too long.

Wait! The Cougar Club chatters!

Night had fallen, and darkness surrounded her. She glanced at her alarm clock. Nine-thirty. Would anyone be in the chatroom on a Sunday night? Of course, the other day she had logged on at midnight and three women were there.

It couldn't hurt to try.

Still hugging her pillow laced with Jack's musky fragrance, she wandered into her office and fired up the computer.

MrsRobinson: *Holly, good evening! Nice to see you again. Afraid it's just you and me tonight. Sundays are usually pretty low key.*

Holly typed frantically, correcting typos as she went.

HollyGolightly: *I'm so glad someone's in here. I really need to talk.*

MrsRobinson: *Talk away. That's what I'm here for.*

Where did she begin? She sat and tapped the spacebar for what seemed like hours.

MrsRobinson: *You still there?*

HollyGolightly: *Yes.*

MrsRobinson: *You're safe here, Holly.*

Safe. That's what ILoveCubs had told her the first time

she'd wandered into this chatroom. Safe. She could tell her story. Tell it to someone who might understand. MrsRobinson's name was Megan, wasn't it?

HollyGolightly: *May I call you Megan?*

MrsRobinson: *Of course. Is your real name Holly?*

HollyGolightly: *Yes.*

MrsRobinson: *What's going on? I'll help if I can.*

Holly inhaled deeply and blew the air out in a slow stream. Megan couldn't help. No one could. But at least she could listen. Holly had never said these things out loud. But for the first time, she needed to get it all out.

HollyGolightly: *I met a man. A wonderful man. He's 29, and I'm 40. I didn't mean to fall in love with him, but I couldn't help it. He's nothing like I imagined he'd be. We actually met on a one-night stand. Something I never do...*

MrsRobinson: *Why did you do it that time, then?*

Holly sighed. The million dollar question.

HollyGolightly: *I was in a bad place. I had*

just been diagnosed with cervical cancer.

There, she'd said it.

MrsRobinson: *I'm so sorry, Holly. Are you okay now?*

Okay? Physically, sure, she was okay. A picture of health, in fact. But emotionally? A wreck.

> **HollyGolightly:** *Yes. It hadn't spread, thank God. I didn't need any radiation or chemo. They got it all.*

Yes, they had gotten it all, but at what cost?

MrsRobinson: *I'm so glad to hear that.*

> **HollyGolightly:** *Problem is, they did a hysterectomy. I got to keep one ovary, to keep my hormones balanced, but other than that, I'm empty. I've never been married, never had kids. I had to accept that I never would.*

MrsRobinson: *I'm so sorry, Holly.*

> **HollyGolightly:** *I tried to look at the bright side. I was alive. They'd caught it in time to cure me. I'd gone this long without kids, and my biological clock was ticking anyway. I wasn't in a relationship, so what did it matter? I figured any man I'd get involved with would*

> *probably have kids by now anyway. At least*
> *those are the things I told myself.*
> *Do you have kids, Megan?*

It was a while before she answered. Holly knew Megan was pitying her, which annoyed her.

MrsRobinson: *Two girls.*

> **HollyGolightly:** *You must be very proud*
> *of them.*

MrsRobinson: *I am. They're both in college now.*

> **HollyGolightly:** *So you're divorced?*

MrsRobinson: *From their father, yes. I'm remarried. To my cub.*

> **HollyGolightly:** *How old is he?*

MrsRobinson: *He's forty, and he never wanted kids. He's a wonderful stepfather, though. Joy and Laurie adore him.*

So Megan had gotten lucky and found herself a cub who didn't want kids. Holly cleared her throat and began to type.

> **HollyGolightly:** *When Jack—that's his*
> *name—came back into my life out of the blue,*
> *I didn't want to get involved. I knew I could*

never give him what he deserved—a family.
He was very persistent and so attractive.
I caved. Now I'm in too deep.

MrsRobinson: *Have you told him the truth?*

HollyGolightly: *No. I can barely think about*
it myself. This is the first time I've talked
to anyone about it.

MrsRobinson: *You need to tell him.*

HollyGolightly: *It's too late now. I hung*
on way too long without telling him. He has
a son, you know. An adorable kid. Six years
old. Was never married to the mom and she's
not in the picture. When I found out, I was
ecstatic. I figured maybe he'd be okay with
not having more kids. That's not the case.

MrsRobinson: *How did you find out?*

HollyGolightly: *Eating breakfast with*
his kid. He told me he really wanted a little
brother, and that his dad had told him maybe
someday. That pretty much takes me out of
the picture. Which I knew from the beginning.
This is my own fault for getting in so deep.
But now...

She couldn't finish the sentence so she hit enter. Tears had blurred the computer screen.

MrsRobinson: *Now what, Holly?*

Holly sniffed and wiped her eyes with the back of her hand. Where was her damned box of tissues?

HollyGolightly: *Now I've involved his son. He'll be hurt. His son will be hurt. And I'll be hurt. I should have ended it before now. Then I'd be the only one hurting. God knows I've dealt with that before, and I could have dealt with it again.*

MrsRobinson: *There's still time to salvage this, Holly. If this man loves you, he won't care that you can't give him another child.*

HollyGolightly: *He never said he loved me.*

MrsRobinson: *But you love him.*

With all her heart.

HollyGolightly: *Yes.*

MrsRobinson: *Then how can you give up? You have to try. Tell him the truth.*

HollyGolightly: *Can it work, Megan? This whole cougar thing? I don't know. I mean, twenty years from now he'll be in his prime, and I'll be an old lady.*

MrsRobinson: *First of all, sixty is not an old*

lady. Not anymore. And yes, it can work. I'll grant you that I got lucky, finding a cub who wasn't interested in having children.

HollyGolightly: *When I was in here the other night, Charlene's relationship was ending because her cub wanted a family and she was done with that.*

MrsRobinson: *Yes, that does happen sometimes. I can't lie to you. But you're a little bit ahead of Charlene. Your Jack already has a child.*

HollyGolightly: *But he wants more.*

MrsRobinson: *Are you sure about that?"*

HollyGolightly: *That's what his son said.*

MrsRobinson: *But you've never had this conversation with him?*

HollyGolightly: *No.*

MrsRobinson: *You need to. Talk to him. If he cares for you, he'll listen. Maybe you can find a way to compromise.*

HollyGolightly: *How? I can't give him a child.*

MrsRobinson: *It's not all black and white, Holly. You can adopt. And you still have an* *ovary. If you really want a child of your own body, you can try in vitro fertilization with a surrogate. There are many ways to have children these days.*

> **HollyGolightly:** *But I'm so old! I'd be sixty when the kid graduated high school.*

MrsRobinson: *Sounds like you already wrote the whole thing off.*

> **HollyGolightly:** *I kind of had to, when I got my diagnosis. I had to accept that I'd never be a mother. Then Jack came along again, and I found myself wanting something that I thought I'd closed the door on.*

MrsRobinson: *Why didn't you just tell him the truth from the beginning?*

Good question. Why hadn't she?

> **HollyGolightly:** *I honestly don't know.*

MrsRobinson: *Were you afraid he'd leave you?*

> **HollyGolightly:** *I never thought of it in those terms. I always knew I'd have to leave him eventually.*

MrsRobinson: *So you made the choice for him.*

HollyGolightly: *I guess I did.*

MrsRobinson: *Then you've sold him short. Let him decide. The worst he can do is break it off, and you'll be no worse off than you are now.*

True enough. Why hadn't she thought of it in this way? Because she'd been too busy feeling sorry for herself and too busy being selfish. She'd strung Jack along because she couldn't bear to say goodbye. Then she'd escaped in a haze of cowardice when the going got rough. No more.

HollyGolightly: *You're absolutely right, Megan. Thank you so much! I'm going to call him right now.*

MrsRobinson: *Yes! Let me know how it works out. I'll cheer for you if you have good news and I'll hold your hand if it's bad. That's what we're here for.*

HollyGolightly: *You're a gem. I'll log back on when I have news.*

She hurriedly logged off, a spark of energy radiating throughout her. She grabbed her cell phone out of her purse, and then stopped abruptly.

She didn't have Jack's number.

All this time, and she hadn't thought to get his number.

How had she fallen head over heels for a man and not gotten his phone number?

She'd truly lost her mind. And her heart.

Calling information proved fruitless. He was unlisted. She didn't know Luisa's last name, either, so she couldn't call her. She did, though, have Mark's cell number and email on her course syllabus. He'd said his students could contact him anytime. She checked her watch. Somehow, she knew he hadn't meant she could call him at ten thirty at night.

She'd have to wait until morning. She hoped she wouldn't lose her nerve by then.

CHAPTER TWELVE

Jack sat in his son's room, watching the methodic rise and fall of the little boy's chest as he breathed. When Sam had first come to him, only a little over three months old, Jack had been terrified of SIDS. He'd kept the baby in a cradle in his own bedroom, close enough to reach over and touch the little chest whenever he woke during the night. The rhythmic up and down motion had soothed him then.

The time had long since passed for Jack to worry about his boy making it through the night. But still, on nights when his mind whirled and wouldn't let him sleep, he'd sneak into Sam's bedroom, place his hand over his son's chest, and let the soft cadence of his breathing—his life force—comfort him.

He'd never known what it was like to love a person more than himself until Sam had come into his life. That tiny little person had crept into his heart and grasped it with those chubby little hands, until Jack wondered if his heart had room for anyone else.

During the last week, he'd discovered how spacious his heart actually was. Holly had sneaked in. Somehow, she'd uncovered the key. Jack hadn't planned to fall in love with her. Yet, when he brought her into his home and introduced her to his son, he'd known she was the one.

The one he'd been searching for his whole life. He just hadn't let it materialize on a conscious level.

He sighed and gently laid his palm on his son's chest. He

loved this child more than anything. He'd die for his little boy. If anyone dared to harm him? Such a perpetrator had better look to God for forgiveness, for he'd get none from Jack.

Sam's heartbeat fluttered beneath Jack's fingertips and his chest rose and fell with each shallow breath of sleep.

Holly had hurt Sam.

Sam had wandered into the barn during midmorning, his big brown eyes wide and confused. "Luisa says Holly left."

Jack had turned from his chore. "What?"

"Yeah. She was supposed to go riding with us again but she left."

"Oh, God." Jack's heart had plummeted to his stomach. Something was wrong. She wouldn't just...take off.

"How'd she go? She doesn't have her car."

"Carlos took her."

He had scooped Sam into his arms and carried him quickly back to the house. "Luisa!" He slammed the door. "Luisa, where are you?"

She'd come running. "I'm here. Goodness, what's wrong?"

"Where's Holly?"

"She had to go. Carlos drove her home."

"Why? What happened?"

"She just said she was sorry. That something came up."

"Is she okay?"

"Yes. She was fine when she left here. She said she'd call you later."

"Oh. Thank goodness."

"Does that mean she's not goin' ridin' with us today, Daddy?" Sam's big eyes held sadness.

"I'm afraid so, pal," Jack had said, kneeling down to face his son. "But I'm sure she'll come back soon to go ridin'."

"But she promised."

"I know. I'm sure she has a good reason why she can't go today. Tell you what, we'll go ridin' anyway. Just you and me. How does that sound?"

Sam had sniffed. "Yeah, that'd be good I guess."

Jack had spent the rest of the day with his son. His heart drank in the pleasure of being with his little boy. When Sam had fallen asleep to a story of the Old West, he'd had an innocent smile on his face.

He'd finally stopped wondering why Holly hadn't stayed to spend the rest of the weekend.

Jack had taken care of his son, made sure he was happy and unhurt, because that's what a father did.

No one existed to take away Jack's own hurt.

Nearly midnight, and here he sat, watching his son sleep. How was it possible Sam had been so upset by Holly's departure? He'd known her only two days.

Jack understood. Holly had that effect on people. He'd only known her for a little over a week himself, unless he counted their hot one-nighter. That only added ten hours, anyway.

Damn her! Her age had never made a speck of difference to him. That had to be what this was about. How could she disappear without any explanation other than "something suddenly came up?" It sounded like a bad sitcom. Luisa had said it had come out of nowhere. Holly hadn't gotten a phone call or anything. She'd just up and said she needed to go home.

If she'd come to the barn to tell him what had happened, or if she'd even told Luisa, he'd have understood.

But no. She'd just left.

Now she hadn't called.

Jack leaned down and gave his son a quick peck on the cheek. "Sleep tight, pal," he whispered. He tucked the cotton sheet around him a little tighter and left the room.

He fell on his bed, still fully clothed.

It was over.

Hell, it hadn't even begun.

★ ★ ★

Holly looked at her watch. Eight fourteen a.m. Not even a minute had passed since she'd last looked. Was it too early to call Mark? It was Monday, but it was a holiday. He'd given the students his cell number, but he might not appreciate such an early call on a holiday.

Frantically, she picked up her own cell and dialed. Her heart beat like a stampede of buffalo. She'd risk Mark's wrath. She needed to talk to Jack, to tell him how she felt, and why she'd left. *God, please let him understand.*

Five minutes later, Jack's number programmed into her cell, she listened to the ringing on the other end. It wasn't ringing, actually. It was Glen Campbell singing "Rhinestone Cowboy." She couldn't help but smile. Jack hadn't even been alive when that song was popular.

"This is Jack," came his whiskey-smooth voice.

"Jack? It's me."

A pause. A long pause. A pause so fucking long Holly thought for sure the earth had revolved once around the sun already.

Then, finally, "Holly."

She sighed. "Yeah, it's me. Listen, I want to apologize for—"

He cut her off. "Was it an emergency, Holly?"

"Well, not exactly, but—"

"Is someone dead?"

"What?"

"You heard me."

"No. Of course not. No one's dead."

"Anyone in the hospital?"

"No. Jack, just listen—"

"Then there isn't any reason why you couldn't come tell me before you left. Hell, I'd have driven you home. I'd have done anything for you."

Her heart skipped, and tears blurred her vision. "Oh, Jack. Please. I do have an explanation."

"Not one I care to hear."

"But I—"

"Goodbye, Holly."

"Jack!" Had he hung up? *Damn these cell phones! They won't even tell you when someone hangs up on you!*

"Jack! Jack!"

No reply.

A sob broke through, and she threw her cell phone against the wall. It clattered to the ground. She ran to it, relieved it was still intact for the most part. She slid the battery cover back in place and hit redial.

More Glen Campbell.

He didn't answer, and it didn't go to voicemail.

Damn! She tried again. Still no answer.

Now what? She had to talk to him.

She sped into her office and logged in to the Cougar Club. Those ladies would know what to do. No one was chatting. Well, what did she expect? It was before nine a.m. on a holiday morning.

She'd just have to go to Jack's place. She hadn't paid close attention when she'd been driven either way, but if she concentrated...

She took a quick shower, raked her fingers through her wet hair, and added a touch of lipstick. That was it. She didn't want to take any more time. She had to get to Jack before it was too late.

It already is.

She brushed the thought from her mind. True, he might send her packing when he found she couldn't have children, but she had to let him decide. She'd made the decision for him, and that was wrong.

Maybe all he wanted was a casual relationship. Maybe he wasn't in love with her and never would be. Could she live with that?

She sighed and grabbed her purse and car keys from the kitchen counter. No use prognosticating. She'd have all her answers soon enough.

CHAPTER THIRTEEN

"Jack?"

Her voice cut through him like a switchblade. He'd just come in from a midmorning ride with Sam and had sent his son to find Luisa. Taking care of the horses soothed his mind, so he let Sam off the hook this once and decided to curry both horses himself. He'd just finished cleaning the last hoof when her voice sliced into him.

He didn't turn.

"What do you want?"

"I need to talk to you."

"Not interested."

Such a lie. He was so interested that his heart was thundering against his sternum just at the damn sound of her voice. Why had this happened? Why had he fallen in love? Why had he brought her here and introduced her to Sam?

Sam deserved better.

"I'm so sorry..."

Her words trailed off, and he still didn't turn. If he looked at her, he'd be lost.

Her breathy sigh caressed the back of his neck. She was that close. *Don't turn around, Jack.*

"I didn't think you'd get this hurt."

Damn. Those were fighting words. He turned around, and the moistness in her emerald eyes tugged at him. But he hardened his heart.

"Not get hurt? What did you think I invited you here for, Holly? Sex? A prolonged weekend of hedonism? Hell, I didn't need to bring you to my home, introduce you to my son, for that."

"No, I—"

"Please go away."

"I can't, Jack. Not until you hear me out. I behaved stupidly. I know that. But there are reasons. And I—"

He let out a sigh and rolled his eyes. "Yes, I know. You're forty. You've made it abundantly clear how you feel about our age difference. And I thought I'd made it abundantly clear that I don't give a rat's ass, but you can't seem to get past that."

"You don't understand. There's more."

"Nothing I'm interested in." He steeled his heart against her misty green gaze.

"You've got to listen to me."

"I don't have to do anything. Now if you'll excuse me, I need to take care of my animals."

He turned, but she grabbed his arm. A sizzling current traveled to his groin at her touch. She flung her arms around him, grabbed his cheeks, and drew his lips to hers.

His memories soared to their first kiss in the elevator. She nibbled at his lower lip and then his upper, her tongue probing for entrance.

He granted it. Hell, he was still a man—a man in love with a woman. His body couldn't help but respond to her physical presence.

He parted his lips, and when her tongue touched his, he melted and his resolve disintegrated.

She tasted of vanilla cream and still a touch of lime. He devoured her mouth. His mind clouded, and energy—hot, raw, and primal—crackled between them.

He gripped her ass, squeezing, kneading, and forced her against the hardness beneath his jeans. Her tiny moans hummed against the back of his throat and he probed farther, deeper, until he was lost in the passion that had sizzled between them since their first meeting.

Then, from somewhere in a different dimension, a small voice broke through the haze.

"Holly! You came back!"

Jack ripped his mouth from Holly's to stare at Sam. Holly wiped her mouth with the back of her hand and turned.

"Why, hi there, Sam."

"You missed our ride yesterday."

"Yeah, I know. I'm sure sorry about that. Maybe we can go this afternoon."

"Holly, stop," Jack said. He would not allow her to get Sam's hopes up again. He took a deep breath and willed his nerves to settle. Sam was the most important consideration. His only consideration.

Holly gazed up at him, her lips swollen and scarlet. Damn, she was beautiful. He wanted to grab her again and kiss her until he elicited a promise from her that she'd never leave them.

But he'd be strong.

"Run along, Sam. Holly and I need to talk about grown-up things."

"What kinds of things are those?"

"When you're older, I'll explain it. Go on now. Luisa should have lunch ready soon."

"But that's why I came out here, Daddy. Lunch is on the table."

"Tell Luisa I'll be a little late. You go on and eat."

"Okay." Sam trotted off. The kid never walked. He always trotted or ran.

Jack smiled.

"Jack..."

"What?"

"Maybe you should eat first, and then we'll talk."

"Not a chance. You tell me what you came to tell me. And no more kissin' until it's all out in the open."

"So you're ready to listen now?"

He nodded. That kiss had told him what he already knew. He wasn't ready to give her up. Not by a long shot. So he'd listen. But he'd listen from a distance. He picked up the curry comb and got back to his horse.

"You stay there," he said, "and start talkin'."

"This isn't easy for me."

"It isn't for me, either. Last night sucked, Holly. If you think you're the only one hurtin' here, think again."

"I'm sorry."

"Quit apologizin' and explain yourself. I'm agein' here."

She let out a heavy sigh. He focused on the horse's shiny coat.

"It is the age thing, but there's more to it than you know." She cleared her throat. "That first night we met, I told you I was in a bad place."

"I know. We've all been in bad places, Holly."

"This was a particularly bad one, Jack. I'd just been diagnosed with cancer."

Oh, God. His heart dropped to his stomach. He tossed the currycomb to the ground and hurried toward her. "Sugar, are you all right?"

"Yeah, yeah, I'm fine." She swiped her hand across her

nose and sniffed. "Sort of."

"What do you mean, sort of? Sugar, please, tell me you're okay."

"I am. I mean, my life's not in danger or anything."

"Come sit with me." He led her out of the stable and onto a patch of soft grass. He sat down and drew her into his lap. His heart ached.

"Tell me."

"It was cervical cancer, Jack. I-I always had my pap smears, which was lucky. They caught it real early. But it was an aggressive strain. So they treated it aggressively."

"Oh." His heart sank. He already knew where this was going.

"They took my uterus. Plus one ovary. Just left me one for hormones. I'm pretty much cleaned out."

"God."

"I had to give up my dream of being a mom. I thought I'd come to terms with it. Until you came back into my life."

He swallowed and kissed the top of her head. He'd thought about having a child with her. Sure, she was older, but not too old. Now that wouldn't happen.

Did it matter? Sam wanted a brother. He knew that. He sure loved kids and always thought he'd have more eventually, once the right woman came along.

That the right woman might not be able to give him children hadn't occurred to him.

She rested her head against his shoulder and he inhaled the apple-fresh scent of her hair.

"Sugar?"

"Hmm?" Her voice was muffled.

"I never saw a scar."

She lifted her head. "They used a laparoscope. The scar's hidden in my belly button. It's a lot less invasive. I was able to recover a lot quicker."

"Oh." So she had recovered quickly. Physically. He had a hunch she wasn't completely recovered emotionally.

She'd had to give up her dream of children. Could he give up his dream of a child with her?

Before he could formulate an answer to his own question, a scream rent through the air.

Sam!

He stood quickly, his heart hammering, steadying Holly so she didn't fall.

"That's Sam," he said. "Sam! Sam!"

The scream had been loud. He was close by. Jack ran around the stable. Nothing. Across a small field stood the main barn. On the ground, next to a stack of hay bales, lay his son.

He wasn't moving.

"No! Sam! Sam!"

He raced across the field, tears forming in his eyes. Not Sam. Not Sam.

He knelt over the unmoving body of his son. Had he fallen? Jack looked up. He'd tumbled from the roof of the barn. What the hell had he been doing? He was supposed to go in for lunch.

"Jack." Holly knelt beside him. "What happened?"

"I don't know. He fell, I think." His voice sounded peculiar, like it had come from somewhere else. Thoughts couldn't form. He reached under his little boy's body and gently cradled him to his chest.

"Jack, you shouldn't move him. He might be...injured inside."

Jack knew. But he couldn't think. He had to hold his son. He pressed his fingers to his neck. His pulse was steady and strong, thank God.

"I'll call 9-1-1."

"No. No. That'll take too long. I'll drive him to the hospital."

"Jack, be sensible..."

"Damn it, Holly! This is my child! I need to take care of him!"

"I understand." Holly nodded. "I'll drive you."

CHAPTER FOURTEEN

What was taking so damn long?

Holly sat in the ER waiting room and fidgeted with an old *People* magazine.

Jack was in the back with Sam. He'd regained consciousness for a few seconds in the car, said something about a kitty, and then floated back away. He most likely had some broken bones. At least that's what Holly hoped. Bones could be fixed. If he was bleeding inside...

She couldn't go there. What would Jack do without his son? What would she do? She'd grown to care for the little boy in just two days. She loved him, just as much as she loved his father.

An hour passed, and then another. The nurse at the reception desk told Holly, very nicely, to please stop asking for an update. She'd tell her something when she knew.

Holly resisted the urge to smack her.

Just as Holly picked up her fifth magazine, Jack, looking like he'd aged a decade, walked into the waiting room.

She rose from her chair, her purse and magazine flopping to the floor. "Jack?"

He sighed. "He's okay."

She threw her arms around his neck and hugged him close. "Thank God. Come sit with me and tell me what happened."

"I don't know yet. I haven't gotten a straight story out of Sam. But he did wake up for a little while. He has a concussion."

Holly nodded. He looked so sad, so forlorn, and yet so relieved. She shared his sentiment.

"His femur's cracked. The doc was amazed he didn't have more broken bones. He won't need surgery, but he'll wear a cast for a few months. They did an MRI and a CT scan." Jack sighed. "No internal bleeding, thank God."

Holly let out a breath she hadn't realized she'd been holding.

"He's resting now. They have him pretty doped up. He's going to be in a lot of pain. The bruises are already forming all over his little body..." Jack stared at the white wall of the waiting room.

Holly gently cupped his cheek and turned his face to her. "Will he stay the night?"

"Yeah. I'm stayin' with him. I can't leave him alone."

"I understand."

"Could you...?" He sighed. "This is a lot to ask, Holly.

"You can ask me anything."

"Would you mind driving back to the ranch and getting some stuff for me? A change of clothes, my toothbrush, you know."

"Not at all. I'd do anything for you and Sam. I hope you know that."

"I appreciate it."

"Are you hungry? I can get you something."

"No." He rested his elbows on his thighs and cupped his face in his hands. "I can't eat."

"You should eat something. You probably haven't eaten since breakfast." She checked her watch. "It's nearly five."

"Can't. Not hungry."

"All right." She'd bring him something anyway. "It's a long

drive to your place. I won't be back for a few hours. Have you called Luisa?"

"No. Would you?"

"Sure."

Holly quickly programmed the number Jack gave her into her cell. "I'll call her on the way home."

Home? When had she started thinking of Jack's place as home? He hadn't said he loved her. She hadn't told him yet. Now wasn't the time.

She grabbed her purse and gave the top of his head a kiss. "I'll be back as soon as I can."

"I should have been with him," Jack mumbled. "I sent him off to eat lunch so I could talk to you. He should have been my first priority."

"Oh, Jack, sweetheart. How many times have you sent Sam off to have lunch?"

He nodded. "I know. And nothing ever happened. But this time..."

Holly smoothed Jack's rumpled hair. "Don't blame yourself. Please. He's going to be all right. Just thank God for that and move on, okay?"

He nodded into his hands.

Holly knelt in front of him and lifted his face to meet her gaze. "This isn't your fault." It wasn't. It was hers. It was hers for leaving in the first place and then coming back. She'd kept his attention away from his son.

No, she couldn't think like that. It was no one's fault. Things happened. Her cancer had been no one's fault.

She leaned forward and brushed her lips lightly across his. Maybe this was the time, after all. She thumbed his stubbled cheek and kissed him again. "I love you," she whispered against his mouth.

Before he could respond, she escaped the waiting room.

★ ★ ★

He'd murmured a husky "thank you" when she left his bag of clothes and sundries. He'd looked at the container of Italian takeout with glazed eyes, but she'd thrust it into his hands anyway.

"What do you need, Jack?" she'd asked. "I'll do anything for you. For Sam. I'll stay here all night if you want."

He'd shaken his head. "Just go home. I need to be alone with my son."

She'd left, her heart in her throat. He hadn't told her he loved her. Perhaps he didn't. It served her right, anyway.

Now she sat in front of her computer, staring at the blank Cougar Club chatroom. It was nearing midnight on a holiday. Of course no one would be there. They were probably all with their cubs, having a high old time.

Holly drew in a deep breath, flicked off her computer and padded into her bedroom. She flopped onto her bed and cried into the pillow that smelled like Jack.

★ ★ ★

The next few days passed in a fog. Holly went to work, came home, and cried herself to sleep. She skipped both her art classes, something she never did. Her heart wasn't in it.

No word from Jack. She'd tried calling him several times, only to get the endless wails of Glen Campbell. Why didn't he have voicemail? Didn't everyone have voicemail these days? Still, she called.

Her mind buzzed with unlikely scenarios. What if Sam had taken a turn for the worse? What if the doctors had been wrong, and he'd been bleeding internally? And they'd found it too late?

Nausea churned in her belly.

Damn it! She loved that little boy too. Why didn't Jack at least call her to tell her how Sam was doing?

If Jack had decided to let her go, she could live with that. She had no choice, but she needed to know Sam was okay.

Enough was enough. Friday afternoon, she left her office early and drove home to pack a bag. She was driving out to Jack's ranch. He might tell her to take a hike, but by God she'd know if he and Sam were all right. Fear gnawed at her during the long drive out of town.

She gathered her courage as she pulled into the long driveway at Jack's ranch house. Was she sticking her nose in where it didn't belong? Was his indifference his polite way of telling her to get lost?

She breathed in. It was possible, but it didn't matter. She had to know Sam was okay.

Leaving her bag in the car—she didn't want to appear too eager—she trudged to the door and knocked.

She pasted a smiled on her face when Luisa answered.

"Holly, *buenos dias.*"

"Hello, Luisa."

Luisa looked behind her. "Where's Jack?"

"Jack? Why would he be with me?"

Holly craned her neck and peeked behind Luisa into the kitchen. A smiling Sam—his right leg in a full-length blue cast—struggled forward on crutches.

"Holly!" his little voice piped.

"Sit back down, *mijo,*" Luisa scolded. "You must take it easy for the first few days. Remember what the doctor said."

Holly rushed past Luisa and knelt in front of Sam. "I've been worried sick about you. Are you all right?"

"I'm fine. It doesn't hurt so much anymore. Daddy gives me pills." He leaned against her and held out one of his crutches. "Aren't these things neat?"

Holly nodded, a tear forming in the corner of her eye. "Yes, Sam. They are very neat." She pulled the little boy into her arms and gave him a gentle hug.

"So where's Daddy?" Sam asked.

Strange. Luisa had asked the same thing.

"I don't know, sweetie."

"But he went to get you."

A wave of joy swept through Holly. "To get me? What for?"

"To bring you home, he said. Said he'd be back in time for supper, too. Luisa's makin' enchiladas."

Bring her home? Did that mean...? Could she have passed him on the highway?

Her fingers glued to her lips, she turned to Luisa.

"He's right. Jack went for you."

"I didn't think... I mean, he didn't answer any of my calls."

"He didn't get any calls, Holly," Sam said. "But that's kinda my fault. I threw up on his cell phone. One of the pills made me sick. He had to throw it in the garbage."

Holly burst into a giggle. Poor little Sam, sick to his tummy, puking on his dad's cell phone. She stared at his rosy cheeks and big brown eyes. Thank God he was fine now.

Still, Jack could have called her. On the other hand, he'd been busy with Sam, who had no doubt needed his full attention. But one little phone call...

Stop it, Holly. He was focused on his son, and you could have come clean long before you did. He wouldn't have gone for you if he didn't care.

"Do you remember what happened that day, Sam? Why you fell from the roof of the barn?"

"Yeah. One of the kitties was on the roof crying. I had to get him."

"Goodness me," Holly said, hugging him again. "Your dad told you to go in for lunch."

"I know but—"

She smiled into his curly dark hair. "It's okay, Sam. All that matters is that you're okay now."

"I hope Daddy gets back soon."

"I do, too." Holly kissed his ruffled curls. He smelled like fruity shampoo and little boy. A ripple of motherly love surged into her. She loved this child. She wanted to protect him and take care of him.

"He's driving up now," Luisa said, looking out the front window.

Holly lurched forward and steadied Sam against her. "You do as Luisa says," she told him. "Take it easy. Rest. There'll be time for walking on your crutches once you're a little stronger. I'll go say hi to your daddy."

"Okay."

She helped him to the couch in the front room and then whisked past Luisa and out the front door.

Jack stepped from his pickup, her painting in his hand.

Suddenly shy, she slowed to a snail's pace. But when he lifted his lips in that gorgeous smile, she ran into his arms.

He placed the painting on the ground leaning against a

front tire and embraced her with strong and muscular arms. She inhaled the crisp combination of sandalwood, spice, and man that was uniquely Jack and sobbed against his shoulder.

"Shh," he whispered. "Don't cry, sugar."

"When you didn't answer my calls, I thought..."

He chuckled against her cheek. "Didn't have a phone."

She sniffed. "Yeah, I heard. But you didn't call me, either."

"No, I didn't. I'm sorry."

She shook her head against his cotton shirt. "You don't have to be sorry, Jack. All the 'sorrys' belong to me, I'm afraid. And I am sorry. About everything."

"I know." He pushed her away, just a bit, wiped a tear from her cheek, and then tipped her chin upward with his finger. "I missed you."

"Oh, Jack, I've missed you, too."

"I had some thinkin' to do, Holly."

She nodded. "I understand."

He brushed his lips against hers. "I've never come so close to losin' someone I love so much."

"I was so worried about Sam, Jack. That's why I came out here. I... I wanted to see you, of course. I figured you might not want to see me. Still, I needed to know Sam was all right."

"He's going to be just fine."

"I'm so relieved. He's a wonderful little boy."

"Got to agree with you there."

She smiled, and he kissed her again. Just a light brush of lips, but energy sizzled through her veins.

"So"—she cleared her throat—"about that thinking you did?"

"I can't lose Sam, Holly."

"I know that."

"And I can't lose you."

Her heart fluttered. "I don't want to lose you, either."

"Your age never made a difference to me. But I have to tell you, I did always think I'd have more kids."

Another tear meandered down her hot cheek.

"I did a lot of thinkin' about that, while Sam was laid up in the hospital. He slept a lot, and I had all this time to play over all the scenarios of how my life might be. All kinds of things went through my mind, but Sam was always there."

"Of course he was."

"I mean, in the scenarios in my mind."

"I know that's what you meant."

He nodded, and his beautiful face shone with emotion. "My boy was always there, and so were you, Holly."

Warmth coursed through her, and she smiled into his dark eyes.

"Like I said," he continued. "I always thought I'd have more kids. But Sam's enough for me, and I'm hopin'..." He inhaled, looked upward for a split second, and then settled his gaze back on hers. "That is, I'm hopin' maybe Sam might be enough for you, too. I'd like you to be a permanent part of our lives."

"Oh, Jack!" She cupped his cheeks—how wonderful the stubble felt against her fingers—and pulled his lips to hers. The kiss was deep, raw, possessive, and she reveled in the pure joy of it.

When Jack pulled away, she whimpered.

"There's something I need to tell you."

"Then will you kiss me some more?"

"Forever, if you'll let me. I love you, Holly." He fell to one knee and pulled a velvet box out of his pocket. "This was my grandmother's ring, and I'd be honored if you'd accept it. I want you to be my wife. Sam's mother. Will you have us?"

Fresh urgency spiked into her, coupled with a love so fierce she could no longer contain it.

She knelt beside him, and he placed the ring on her left hand.

"I love you, Jack. And I love Sam. I would love nothing more than to spend the rest of my life with the two of you." She leaned into him and kissed the rough stubbled skin below his ear. "You've given me back my dream."

"And you've given me mine."

He lowered his lips to hers and kissed her.

Calendar
BOY

CHAPTER ONE

"I can sign that for you."

Warm breath caressed Stacy Oppenheimer's neck. She turned and looked into smoky hazel eyes—the smoky hazel eyes of the cover model she'd been ogling in the *Men of Romance* Calendar on display at the table outside the Vampire Ball party she was scared to enter. She gripped the stem of the martini glass holding what was left of her cosmopolitan. Nerves! Drove her crazy. An erotic romance writer shouldn't be shy, but she was a classic introvert.

Why enter a party alone when she was frightened to pieces? Why not stare at hot cover models instead? Of course she had gravitated to her favorite, Michael Moretti—six-feet-two-inches of mouth-watering Italian manflesh.

He was known as a womanizer, but God love him, he was the hottest man on the planet.

His gaze dropped to her cleavage.

"Those are..." He smiled and winked. "That's a really nice...shirt."

Her black fishnet top did cling in all the right places. She hadn't bothered with vamp makeup, but she had buried her inhibitions while dressing. The long-sleeved fishnet shirt covered a black satin push-up bra. On her bottom half, she donned a black leather miniskirt.

Yes, womanizer all right. He was thirty-six, she knew, from reading an interview with him on a blog. Older for a cover model and for an exotic dancer, which was his other line of work. With looks like his, though, he'd no doubt flourish in the industry for decades to come. A few silvery strands threaded through his shoulder-length sable hair. Stacy was secretly glad he'd chosen not to cover them. They oozed sex appeal, just like the rest of him.

Still, at thirty-six, he was way too young for her. She was three months shy of her forty-sixth birthday.

Forty-six and alone and scared of her own shadow since her ego-slashing divorce a year and a half ago. Men were more trouble than they were worth. Especially the one staring at her 36 Ds, gorgeous though he may be. He wasn't interested in her. He was a cover model who was paid to be at this conference—paid to make sure authors like her had a great time. If that meant telling them they looked good, he'd do it.

So what the heck? She gulped the rest of her liquid courage—it was her second cosmo—and decided to swallow her nerves and play a little.

She stuck out her chest. "You like them?" She leaned toward Michael, standing on her toes to whisper in his ear. "They're *real*."

His full red lips curved into the dimpled smile she adored. "No way."

He turned and grabbed a vampire clad in Armani coming toward them. Upon closer look under the stage makeup, Stacy recognized him as Dino, another cover model.

"She says those are real," Michael said to the other man.

Dino eyed Stacy's chest as warmth crept to her cheeks. Why had she started this again?

After an eternity, Dino spoke. "I believe her. Good support and all."

Michael smiled again and shook his head, his eyes gleaming. "Real." He glanced down at her hand. "You're married."

Was that disappointment in his voice? She wore a diamond ring, but it hadn't come from her husband. Make that ex-husband. Very, *very* ex. The ring had been her grandmother's, and it didn't fit her right ring finger. She'd always meant to have it resized but never seemed to get around to it. "Oh—" Her shyness kicked in. How did one explain this?

Michael didn't wait for her response. Instead, he eyed her chest once again. "I bet your husband loves them." He picked up her left hand and placed a moist kiss on her ring finger, just above the gem. "Very nice to meet you"—he gazed at her name tag—"Stacy Summers."

Her pen name. Who wanted to read erotic novels by anyone named Oppenheimer? In a flash, he'd walked through the doorway into the Vampire Ball.

Stacy stood alone, her heart racing. Her finger tingled where his lips had brushed softly against her flesh, and her chest and tops of her breasts prickled with red heat. The din of authors chatting as they grazed around the promotion tables buzzed in her ears like white noise.

"Hey, Stacy, what are you standing around here for?"

She jolted out of her stupor to see Veronica Miles, a young unpublished author she had met in a workshop that morning. With gorgeous mocha skin, dark brown eyes, and spectacular curves—not to mention she was at least fifteen years Stacy's junior—Veronica would no doubt be the belle of the ball.

"I was...just getting ready to go in." Stacy inhaled, willing her nerves to settle.

"What are you waiting for, girlfriend?" Veronica grabbed

her arm and pulled her through the doorway. "I hope there are some good tables left. Great outfit, by the way."

"Thank you. You look amazing."

Veronica wore a black sheath that accentuated every spectacular curve of her young, fit body. She hadn't used vampire make up on her dark complexion, and she was stunning.

No use pining over Michael Moretti. If he ever looked Stacy's way again, which was doubtful, he'd see Veronica, and it would be all over anyway.

Still, Stacy was glad Veronica had happened by. Entering a party became much easier with a friend by her side.

"Are you enjoying the conference?" Veronica asked as they scoped the room for some empty chairs.

"Yes, I am. Are you?"

"It's been incredible!" Veronica's husky voice nearly bubbled. "I've met some great people, and I've learned so much. I can't wait to be published."

Stacy smiled. "It will happen soon."

"I hope so."

"If you need any help, let me know. I'd be happy to look at some of your work."

"Would you?" Veronica squeezed her forearm. "I'd so appreciate that."

"Sure, anytime. I gave you my card this morning, right?"

"Yeah."

"Just email me."

"Oh, you're the best, Stacy. There's a table over there." The young woman dragged Stacy along to a table full of younger, hipper people.

"Hi, I'm Veronica, and this is Stacy. Are these seats taken?"

The table of women urged them to sit down, and soon Veronica was chatting away as if they'd all known each other forever. Stacy watched her in action, mesmerized. How she envied extroverts! Why did this come so naturally to people like Veronica, while people like Stacy struggled to feel comfortable?

"So what do you write, Stacy?" one of the others asked.

Stacy cleared her throat and attempted a smile. "Mostly erotic urban fantasy and paranormal. How about you?"

"Male/male," the other author said.

"Oh." Stacy didn't know how to respond. She'd never understood the male/male craze among straight women, but many authors had made it big in the genre.

"Look!" Veronica gestured. "Here come some luscious males now to inspire you, Dolores."

Stacy turned her head to see Michael Moretti and Dino—did he have a last name?—ambling toward their table.

Dino flipped his black cape, and the silky fabric rippled through the air. "You ladies enjoying the party?"

"Yes, it's loads of fun," Veronica said.

"Perhaps I can make it a little more fun for you." Dino grinned. "Would you care to dance?"

"Thank you. I'd love to."

As Dino led Veronica to the dance floor, Stacy sat, her body tense. Now what? She felt completely out of place, as though the room would swallow her up at any moment and she'd be invisible. Conversation droned around her and threatened to suck her into a vortex.

Classic introvert feelings. She'd always been bashful, but the divorce from David had worsened her symptoms. Still, she had flirted a little with Michael earlier. Maybe hope existed.

Not right now, though. A red-hot desire to escape this situation coursed through her. Would anyone notice if she got up and walked out? Of course not. She was invisible after all.

She slowly rose from her chair.

"Leaving?"

Michael's palm warmed her shoulder.

"Yes. I'm...tired. It's been a long day."

"Not"—his perfect teeth dazzled above his chiseled jawline—"until you dance with me, Stacy Summers."

CHAPTER TWO

Michael Moretti didn't usually bother with married women. Not that he couldn't seduce them. Quite the contrary. He'd done it more than once, but somehow he always heard his mother's shrill Catholic voice in his head during the deed. *She's a married woman! You're no better than your father!* Yep, kind of a woody killer. Strange how that Catholic guilt could still get to him when he hadn't been to mass in twenty years. Every once in a while it occurred to him that he didn't have any issues with some of the other Catholic no-nos—namely sex outside of marriage and use of birth control. Nope, he only heard Mama's voice when he was fucking a married woman, probably because his mother had caught his father in bed with the hot married neighbor when Michael was ten. That was the last time he'd seen the low life.

He held out his hand to a beautiful nymph named Stacy Summers. A beautiful *married* nymph. With cascades of auburn hair and the biggest brownest eyes Michael had ever seen, she was almost worth letting his mother scream in his head as he spent himself inside her lush body. He shook his head to clear it. He had other fish to fry tonight. No time to waste on a woman who couldn't fulfill his ultimate goal.

A dance, though, he had time for.

Her hand was slick with sweat as she shyly took his. Redness crept into her cheeks, down her chest, and onto the plump tops of her breasts showing through the black fishnet she wore. Damn, the woman looked hot. If only she weren't married... He'd love to take her up to his room and free the tigress he knew hid inside her bashful exterior. She'd be an animal in bed. Somehow he just knew.

He led her to the dance floor and took her into his arms. Yes, her body was as soft as he'd imagined and curved in all the right places. If only she didn't have that damned ring on!

Slowly, they swayed to the music. Her body tensed against his. Normally, he didn't talk while he danced, but maybe a little conversation would relax her.

He leaned in, positioned his lips above her earlobe, and inhaled the sweet scent of strawberry. "Your husband's a lucky man."

"Oh." Her voice cracked, and she cleared her throat. "I'm not married."

His cock nearly danced a jig inside his jeans. "You're not? What's with the ring then?"

"It was my grandmother's. She left it to me when she died last year."

He smiled. Did her eyes light up just a little? "You might try wearing it on your other hand, sweetheart."

The redness in her cheeks deepened. His cock hardened.

"Yeah, I know. But it doesn't fit, and I haven't had the time to get it resized yet."

Michael stepped back a little and took both her small hands into his. "It's very pretty. And big too."

"Yeah, Grandma was pretty well off. We were really close."

Sadness laced her big brown eyes. Was that mist forming? Why did he have the sudden urge to draw her to his chest and comfort her? Quickly, he willed his mind to return to his task at hand. *Rich grandma dies, leaves everything to hot unmarried granddaughter.*

Just the ticket.

Michael tipped her chin upward and gazed into her big baby browns. "I'm sorry about your grandma."

She sniffed. "Oh, I'm okay. She was ill. It's better this way. I mean, I miss her, but she was in a lot of pain."

"I'm sorry."

"It's just...it happened at a really hard time. My divorce..."

Divorced. Recently. Possibly looking for a rebound guy. Definitely a candidate for rebound sex.

The ticket, all right.

"I'm sorry, sweetheart." He brushed one thumb across her soft cheek.

"Really, it's okay." She brushed his hand away. "I'd rather not talk about it."

He drew her to his body again, brushed his lips against the softness of her earlobe. "You're fucking beautiful."

Hell, it wasn't even a lie. She was ravishing. Even with her eyes sunken and sad, she lit up the whole damned room.

Her head landed softly on his shoulder, and a quiet "thank you" escaped her throat.

"You want to go someplace else? Get a drink?"

Her head popped up. "You mean leave the party?"

"Yeah. Or we can stay. It would be easier to talk without all the noise, though."

"Can we finish this dance first?"

He chuckled. Without thinking, he leaned forward and kissed her pink cheek. "The song just ended, sweetheart."

"Oh."

More pink flooded her cheeks and neck. Damn, it would be worth it to embarrass her all night, just to see how red that beautiful body would get.

"What are you drinking?"

"Cosmopolitans."

"I'll get you another," he said. "Go wait for me outside. By the table with the calendars where we met before." He smiled and headed to the bar.

★ ★ ★

Stacy tapped her high heel on the smooth tile floor. Her hands were clammy, her skin prickled with goosebumps. What had she been thinking, saying she'd meet Michael Moretti out here for a drink?

She glanced at the calendars on the table. There he was, right on the cover. She liked the shot inside better. The photo on the cover displayed more skin, but the shot inside was a black-and-white, taken in the shower. It showed his amazing back and his broad shoulders, with his hair hanging in wet black waves down his neck. Rather than his whole face, the photo revealed his profile—his chiseled masculine jawline, his perfect aquiline nose—very sexy.

He truly was a god.

Her insides tumbled. Where the hell was he with her drink?

"There you are, beautiful."

His husky voice washed over her like a smooth bourbon. He handed her a cosmopolitan, and to avoid talking, she immediately took a drink of the crisp pink liquid. She took another and another.

"Slow down." Michael touched her forearm.

Her skin sizzled, and she jerked away.

"No hurry. There are plenty of drinks." He arched one eyebrow. "Besides, I want you coherent."

Warmth crept to Stacy's cheeks. "I'm just fine, Mr. Moretti." *Mr. Moretti?* Had she really said that?

"You can call me Michael, beautiful. What shall I call you? Ms. Summers?" His eyes gleamed. "Mistress Stacy?"

Stacy took another gulp of her drink. Mistress? She might write about light bondage occasionally, but she'd never practiced it. Had never wanted to. Her sex life with David had been...sterile. She couldn't think of any other way to describe it. He brushed his teethand then kissed her, moving his tongue methodically in circles for exactly ten minutes. He fumbled with her clit for a minute or two and then shoved his cock inside her before she was wet enough to enjoy it. Afterward, he'd brush his teeth again, wash his cock, come to bed, and turn his back to her.

In twenty years of marriage, he'd never gone down on her. She'd gone down on him the few times he requested it, but he'd never come in her mouth. In twenty years of marriage, she'd never had an orgasm.

Just once, she longed to feel *the amazing momentary sense of floating, the suspension of time, the tingling spreading rapidly from her pussy through her core, to her arms and legs...*

She'd described the female orgasm in so many different ways in her writing, and reviewers often praised her for portraying the woman's sexual experience in such a realistic and sensual way.

What a crock. If the reviewers only knew... Stacy Summers, "the Queen of the female orgasm," as one reviewer had called her, was all theory. She might as well be a virgin for all her practical experience.

She cleared her throat, erasing the sting from the last large gulp of alcohol. "Just Stacy is fine."

"Stacy it is, then. Or I may just call you beautiful, if that's okay."

Another crock, but what the heck? Why not live out a fantasy for a few minutes this evening? She could talk to her favorite cover model, share a drink or two. "Do you want to go sit in the bar with our drinks?" she asked.

"I had something a little more intimate in mind." Michael's tone was teasing as his voice caressed her.

"Intimate?" She willed her voice not to crack. "Like what?"

"Like my room, maybe?"

Stacy shook her head. Had she heard him correctly? No way was she was going to Michael Moretti's room tonight. Granted, he was the hottest thing walking, but he had what must amount to an abundance of sexual experience. He'd expect her, an erotic romance author, to know her way around a man.

She shook her head again. Michael Moretti wasn't coming on to her. What would he want with a middle-aged divorcée? He could have his pick of any sweet young thing here, including the female cover models. Surely he couldn't be suggesting... Of course not.

"I don't think your room is the best idea," she said.

"Well, the bar's kind of noisy."

"It's less noisy than the party."

He chuckled. "True enough. All right, the bar it is." He held out his arm. "At your service, Mistress"—he grinned—"er...Stacy."

Her nerves jittering, she shyly placed her hand in the

crook of his elbow. God, solid muscle... The man couldn't have a gram of fat on his entire body. Of course not, he stripped for a living. When not modeling for covers, he headlined for the Chicago Playboys, an all male revue that rivaled Chippendales in popularity. She briefly wondered if he took steroids to maintain his physique. She hoped not.

Luckily, the bar was only a few hundred yards away. Stacy made it without tripping over her high heels, for which she was eternally grateful. The dimly lit bar was not crowded, most likely because the hotel was filled with conference attendees who were all at the vampire party. Michael found a cozy table for two. He ordered another cosmo for Stacy, who still gripped the one he'd given her in the hallway, and a scotch on the rocks for himself.

"So," he said, once the waitress had left, "tell me about Stacy Summers."

Nothing like laying it right out on the table. Stacy hated talking about herself. Why would anyone find her interesting? "I'm a writer, but I guess you know that," she said shakily.

"I had assumed." His cocky smile lit up his face. "But that can't be all there is to know about such a lovely woman as yourself."

Oh, he was good. He played his part well. No doubt he earned his payment for the weekend because he certainly knew how to charm the ladies. What could she possibly say to him that he would find remotely interesting? "I'm divorced, a little over a year now."

"Yeah, you told me, remember?"

"I did?"

He smiled. "While we were dancing."

Of course. The familiar pink heat crept over her flesh.

God, she was an idiot.

"How long were you married?" he asked

"A while." No way was she going to admit to twenty years in a passionless marriage. That would give away her age.

"Any kids?"

"No. David didn't want kids."

"And you?"

Her? She had longed to be a mother, but in her introverted way, she had agreed to David's desires. Now, at forty-five, she was too old for motherhood. "I was fine with his decision." A lie, but why would Michael care to hear how she'd cried over the loss?

"A shame," Michael said.

She widened her eyes. Why would he say such a thing? "What do you mean?"

He brushed on finger over her forearm. "I mean it's a shame you never had kids. A shame you didn't pass those amazing genes on to the next generation."

Her skin tingled under his touch. "Amazing genes?"

"You're beautiful, Stacy. But I've already told you that."

Oh, yes, he was good, all right. Warmth flooded her cheeks and neck. She had no idea what to say, what to do.

Be Johnny Carson.

Advice from the therapist she'd seen before she and David decided to call it quits. She had complained that she never knew what to say in social situations, that she felt shy, awkward, and conspicuous. The therapist had said, "Be Johnny Carson. Ask the person questions about himself. Everyone likes talking about himself." The only problem was, what to ask?

She took a sip of cosmo. "How about you? Have you ever been married?"

"Nope. Never had the pleasure. I was engaged once. It... didn't work out."

The writer in her sensed a story there, but she couldn't pry. She wasn't that brave. Hell, she wasn't brave at all.

Why was she here again?

"Any kids?"

Shit. Foot in mouth. He'd never been married. How would he have kids?

He lowered his eyes for a second. Was that sadness? When he looked back at her, the question didn't seem to faze him. "Nope. No kids for me either."

"Sorry. You already told me you hadn't been married. That was a stupid question."

The left side of his mouth curved up into a crooked smile. "You don't need marriage to have kids, beautiful. A lot of my friends have them and haven't been married."

"Right. Of course. I just meant..." *God, shut up, Stacy!* She let out a short laugh. "I don't know what the hell I meant."

Michael's finger traveled farther up her forearm and rested in the ticklish spot inside her elbow. "You have a great laugh."

His touch ignited her. "Yeah, and I'm great at saying the wrong thing."

"Listen"—he scooted her chair closer to hers—"why don't you loosen up? Let the real Stacy out? I'd like to get to know her."

"Why do you want to get to know me?" She truly wondered. David had been married to her and had never wanted to "get to know her." "Besides, I'm a lot older than you are."

"Do I look like I care? How old are you, anyway?"

Stacy didn't believe in lying about her age, even to impress the likes of Michael Moretti. "Forty-five."

"Well, you're beautiful. You don't look a day over thirty."

Right. She looked good for her age, she knew, but thirty? "Right."

"I'm not lying, sweetheart. You're hot, and I really do want to get to know you.

"Why on earth would you want to get to know me?"

His hazel gaze penetrated hers. "Because when I first saw you standing there looking at my photograph, I couldn't wait to get you into bed."

CHAPTER THREE

Goosebumps prickled her flesh. Her heart pounded and her tummy somersaulted. A gush of feminine awareness assaulted her from inside.

This is what it felt like—the sexual attraction she wrote about. That initial crackle of energy that passed between a man and a woman, so intense it was almost visible. A hunger, deep and carnal, stirred to life between her legs. A hunger that needed—no, *demanded*—to be sated.

She downed the rest of her cosmo just as the waitress set the drinks Michael had ordered onto the table. The alcohol scorched her throat, warmed her belly, intensified the raw heat growing in her core. She swallowed.

What would Starr do?

Starr Shannon was Stacy's most popular heroine, the lead character in her bestselling erotic urban fantasy series. Readers loved Starr's brashness, her fiery nature. Starr didn't wait around for life to find her, she took what she wanted. She made things happen. She created her own success. When she was attracted to a man, she let him know it. Starr was a sexual dynamo, a multi-orgasmic superwoman.

For just one night, Stacy would be Starr.

"Let's go then."

Michael picked up his scotch and swirled it around a little. The ice clinked against the glass. "Go where?"

"To bed? Isn't that what you want?"

"Uh..."

Was that a blush creeping into his warm olive skin? Could he get any better looking?

"What?"

"Our drinks just got here."

"So what? We'll take them with us." Stacy's heart drummed a rhythmic cadence against her sternum. "Are you a man or an amoeba?"

"Um...a man, I assure you."

Had she actually embarrassed him with that stupid line? It was from a movie, but she couldn't remember which one at the moment. "That's what I thought." She stood and grabbed her drink. "To your room then?"

"I have a roommate. Dino."

"But you wanted to go to your room before."

"For a drink, yeah. Dino's busy at the party. But to get busy... We might get interrupted."

"So you'd rather not *get busy* then?"

"Hell, no! I mean, yes, I want to get busy."

He stood up next to her. Lord, he was tall! So tall and handsome and hot. The heat between their two bodies was palpable. "I can't think of anything else I'd rather do, beautiful."

"Good." She picked up his scotch and handed it him. "My room then."

He took her arm and guided her toward the elevators. "You sure about this?"

Stacy smiled, channeling Starr once again, "I've never been so sure about anything, handsome."

"God..." He led her into an empty elevator. "Which floor?"

"Fifteen."

Michael pressed the button and then leaned toward her.

"I've been dying to kiss those ruby red lips of yours."

She curved her lips into what she hoped was a coy smile. "Nothing stopping you that I can see."

He gently brushed his lips against hers, first in a slow slide and then a tiny nibble across her lower lip. They were both still holding their drinks, and though each had a free hand, only their lips were touching. Very sensual and erotic, even though it was a light teasing kiss. Stacy's insides quivered.

She might be next to a novice when it came to sex, but she did know how to kiss. Luckily, she had done lots of making out before David. She loved to kiss, and she was definitely going to make the most out of kissing such a gorgeous male specimen as Michael Moretti.

When her introverted self threatened to surface, she consciously told herself to bury it. Tonight she was Starr, and Starr would give Michael Moretti a kiss he'd never forget.

She sensed a hint of tightly harnessed control. At least that's what Starr would sense. Stacy had written about such control numerous times. So like Starr in the same situation, Stacy decided to unleash Michael's passion right here in the hotel elevator.

She pressed her lips to his, exerting more pressure, touched her tongue to his upper lip. Such gorgeous full lips! A true pleasure to kiss. The tickle between legs intensified. She could almost feel her labia swelling, her juices accumulating. Oh, this was going to be a wonderful night. A wonderful, pleasurable night. All she had to do was be Starr.

A slow burn of lust curled through her. She tasted the tang of his scotch on his tongue as its tip touched hers. His mouth opened against hers, as if asking permission to take more. With a thrust of her tongue, she granted it, and what had been a light and teasing kiss became passionate, raw, and primal.

Tongues lashed and dueled, lips nipped and ground against each other. Teeth nibbled and bit. She sucked at his lower lip, at his upper, at both together. Her mouth was demanding and greedy, taking all she could with this one kiss.

His groan reverberated against the back of her throat, exciting her even more. Open-mouthed and wet, the kiss went on and on. Liquid spilled from her martini glass and trickled down her arm, and when the elevator dinged its arrival at her floor, she hardly heard it.

Michael tore his mouth from hers, breaking the suction with a loud smack. "We're here."

"Where?"

"Your floor, your room." He pressed his lips to her cheek. "That was some kiss, sweetheart." He took her cosmo. "I think we lost some of our drinks."

"I have more in my room."

"Oh, I don't think we need any more." He winked at her. "I want you completely coherent for what I have planned."

Right, she didn't need alcohol. Starr Shannon didn't drink. Stacy didn't need to drink tonight either. She was feeling warm but not buzzed. Just as well, as Michael said. If this was going to happen, she wanted to remember every single, solitary detail of making love to the hottest man on the planet.

"This way," she said, leading him to room 1543. Quickly, she slid her keycard into the slot and opened the door.

Michael set their half-empty glasses on a table and grabbed Stacy, forcing her against the wall. His mouth opened against her neck, and he sucked her flesh against his lips.

The sweet pressure made Stacy crazy. Her pussy pulsed in time with her heartbeat, and her head swam. Michael's hardness pushed against her belly, and he ground it into her as his lips moved upward. He traced her jawline with tiny kisses and nibbled over the same path.

Nectar gushed between her legs. Her body was on alert. Every sensation seemed magnified.

"You're so amazing, sweetheart. So beautiful."

His words were a slow caress, adding to the sensual agitation already flowing through her.

"I want you so bad, Stacy. So fucking bad."

She opened her eyes. Michael had stopped kissing her, had bent his legs to press his cock against her mound. Her clit throbbed inside her panties. Too many clothes, too many barriers. Her tiny black skirt, her thin panties—it was all too much. She wanted to be naked with Michael. Naked and sexy and nasty.

"I want you too. I want to fuck you. I want to suck your cock. I want you to eat me. Will you eat me, Michael?"

He groaned, and his handsome face contorted into a sensual grimace. He inhaled. "God, I can already smell you. You smell like sex, Stacy. Like sweet sex. I want to bury my face between your legs. I promise I'll eat you until you scream."

She was ready to scream now. He lifted his shirt and threw it on the ground as she toyed with the snap on his jeans. Lord, he'd gone commando. His erection sprang out as soon as she unzipped, and it was more beautiful than she'd ever imagined. She'd described many a penis in her writing, but Michael's golden shaft was worthy of a whole page. Long, thick, and perfectly formed, it stood at attention, ready to pleasure her. Ready to be pleasured.

He fumbled with the edge of her fishnet top, lifting it over her head, stopping to squeeze her full round breasts on the way.

"Perfect," he said. "These are so fucking perfect."

"I told you they're real."

He unsnapped her black push-up bra and pulled it off her, letting it drop to the floor. Her breasts fell gently against her chest.

"God, I believe you." He cupped them, squeezed them. "They're so soft, so pliable. They're real all right. When I thought you were married, I swear to God I thought your husband was the luckiest SOB in the free world to get to lick and suck these every night."

Her body quaked as she readied to channel her character once more. "Well, tonight is your lucky night, handsome. They're all yours."

He groaned and lowered his head, dropping kisses along her cleavage. "You smell like ripe peaches." He cupped one breast, gently teasing the nipple with his index finger.

Stacy gasped as the bud drew up tighter and her areola became taut and wrinkled. When he dipped his head and touched his tongue to the nub, electricity flashed through her.

David hadn't paid much attention to her breasts. And though she'd done her share of making out before David, she'd been a good girl and hadn't let any man venture underneath her clothing. This was the sizzle she'd written about, the amazing sensation of mouth on nipple.

This could go on forever and she would die a happy woman!

She shuddered and whimpered in pleasure. "That feels so good."

"I haven't even begun to make you feel good, Stacy." He closed his lips around the nipple and tugged.

"Oh!" She willingly stopped herself from begging and

decided to go with her feelings, not her thoughts. For the last time, she thought about Starr, and then she consciously decided just to feel. "Yes, Michael, yes. Suck my nipple, just like that."

"Mmm." His voice vibrated against her sensitive flesh. "You're so fucking hot." As he sucked, his fingers crept to her other nipple, and he teased it between two fingers.

The pressure ignited Stacy. "More, Michael. More."

He twisted the hard bud while he nibbled on the other. His cock hung between his legs, hard and inviting, a pearly drop of pre-come glistening on its head. She reached for it, clasped her hand around its thick girth.

He winced. "God, Stacy," he said against her breast. "Not yet."

Had she done something wrong? "I'm sorry."

"Don't be. God." His fingers left her nipple and dived beneath her skirt to rub between her legs. "It's just...I'm so turned on. And fuck, you're *so* wet. Your panties are drenched."

From what she knew, that was a good thing. "I'm wet for you, Michael. I want you."

"Fuck, I want you too, baby. All of you." He withdrew his hand from between her legs and pushed her skirt and panties down with one swoop.

She started to step out of her black strappy sandals, but he stopped her. "Leave them on, baby. They're so sexy. And right now I want to taste that wet pussy of yours."

He led her to the bed. "Lie down on your back," he said, a tone of command in his voice, "and spread those long pretty legs."

His jeans still hanging on his hips, Michael knelt between Stacy's thighs. He closed his eyes and inhaled. "Mmm. I've been smelling you all night, and it's been driving me slowly insane."

Stacy shivered. She wanted this, wanted it more than she wanted to breathe at the moment. No man had ever put his mouth on this part of her, and though she'd written about the ecstasy of oral sex, she knew nothing about it firsthand. How would it feel? Would she shoot to the sky as Starr did? Would she...*come*?

God, she hoped so.

"You're as swollen as a ripe peach, Stacy. Swollen and so pretty down here." He slid his fingers over her wet folds. "So slick and wet for me." He squeezed her labia between two fingers. "Beautiful."

Stacy took a deep breath and closed her eyes. The sensation of his fingers on her private parts was new and exciting, so much more than she had imagined despite what she'd written, and he hadn't even tasted her yet.

Yowza! Sparks blazed across her flesh when he flicked the tip of his tongue against her swollen clit. A low moan escaped her throat.

"Yeah, baby. You like that? I'm going to shove my whole tongue up that hot wet cunt, baby."

Cunt? She used naughty words frequently in her writing, but the c-word was one she'd refused to use. *Cunt*. She mouthed the word, imagined Michael's low husky voice saying it again. *Cunt*. Damn, it was sexy! It turned her on.

"Tell me what you like," he said against her wet flesh. "Tell me how to lick you, to make you hot."

She was already hot. On fire. How could she tell him what she liked when she didn't yet know herself? "I like it all, Michael," she said, her breath coming in rapid pants. "Do it all to me. Lick my...cunt."

Wow, it felt good to say the word! Like a weight had been lifted off her shoulders. With that word part of her introversion melted away, replaced by raw need and desire. The carnal hunger inside her grew and grew.

"You taste amazing," Michael said. He tugged on her labia, plunged his tongue into her passage.

Her whole body ignited. Something was happening, something big. Little pings of pleasure jolted through her each time his tongue hit her clit. The sparks broadened, intensifying, and soon her entire pussy was pulsing. Big. This was fucking big! She breathed rapidly, focusing on the steady need building within her. Part of her longed to break away, escape this mounting gratification. It was too much really, just too much. Time wasn't suspending. She was still fully coherent. But how could the whole world be centered in her pussy? Her hips moved, seemingly of their own volition, matching each stroke of Michael's tongue. He lapped at her, sucked her, and when he forced one finger into her slick channel...

Explosion.

The contractions started inside her but soon encompassed her entire vulva and radiated upward to her belly and chest, outward to her arms and legs. Words left her mouth, words over which she had no control. "Michael...God, Michael...so good...again....again!"

The orgasm rolled through her, and just when she thought the waves were subsiding, they started again. He thrust his fingers in and out of her.

"That's it, baby. Come again. Come for me."

The line between reality and fantasy dimmed as thrill after thrill shot through her. Nothing existed except her and Michael and such intense pleasure she could barely comprehend it. She floated downward gently, and when the contractions finally subsided, she lay still, spent.

A faint kiss on her lips jarred her back to reality. She opened her eyes to see Michael's green-brown gaze locked onto hers.

"You have the softest, sweetest pussy I've ever tasted," he said. He kissed her lips again, tracing them with his tongue. "I haven't even come close to having enough of you."

She smiled against his lips, the zest of her own juices teasing her tongue. Should she tell him that had been her very first orgasm ever? That he'd shown her something amazing that she'd only imagined until now?

No. That would spoil his fantasy, if he had one, of bedding the erotic romance author. She'd play the experienced woman tonight. She'd play Starr.

"Lucky for you then," she said, "because it just so happens that I'm not going anywhere."

CHAPTER FOUR

Christ, she was hot. The lips of her pussy had opened like a flower for him. God, that was so sappy. She was beautiful down there, though, as beautiful as she was everywhere else. And her taste—a mixture of sweet and tart that tantalized his mouth like nothing ever had. Servicing her indefinitely would be no hardship at all. He was hooked, and he hadn't even fucked her yet.

He stood up and removed his shoes and jeans. His cock throbbed. He was so horny. He couldn't wait to sink into her hot cream.

He turned to look at her spread out on the bed like a Renaissance painting. Her reddish-brown hair splayed across the white comforter like flaming tresses. Her crimson lips were slightly parted, glistening and kissable. Long black lashes rested on the tops of her cheeks. Her breasts hung lazily to each side, the nipples rosy from his earlier attentions. Her legs were still parted. The triangle above her treasure was a deeper auburn, and her pussy lips were a shimmering burgundy, still swollen.

He couldn't wait to make her come again. His erection stirred, pulsing. Pre-come oozed from its tip.

Stacy's eyes were closed, but Michael knew she wasn't sleeping. Afterglow. He'd seen it a thousand times, but never had it been more radiant. Her chest rose and fell with each breath, her breasts swaying gently.

For a moment, he thought he could be happy just staring at her.

His cock had other ideas.

As much as he wanted to feel her sweet mouth envelop him, more than anything he wanted to sink inside that pussy. He fumbled in his jeans for a condom, ripped the packet open, and sheathed himself. He moved back toward the bed and gazed at her body sleek with perspiration. A rosy glow. Beautiful.

He sat down next to her and touched between her legs. Mmm, still wet and juicy. He could slide right in.

"Stacy?" he said softly.

The long black lashes framing her big eyes lifted. "Hmm?"

"I want to make love to you. Are you ready?"

"Mmm hmm." She opened her legs a bit more, welcoming him.

Missionary position wasn't his favorite, but right now he couldn't wait. He had to have her. He climbed atop her shimmering body and thrust into her heat.

Her soft sigh made him groan. What was it about this woman? She was beautiful, yes, and her pussy was sweet as clover honey. Yet his craving for her seemed insurmountable. He'd fuck her all night to sate himself if he had to. Anything to get his raw need for her out of his system.

No way was he going to be emotionally dependent on any woman, not even the one taking care of him for the rest of his life.

He pulled out and plunged back in. She was so tight, so warm, so welcoming.

"That feels good, Michael."

"Oh, yes it does." He ground his hips into her in slow

circles, pushing farther and farther into her depths. Then he returned to slow and methodical thrusts.

Sensation filled him, tore across the length of his rigid cock. He pumped harder, faster, the head of his shaft fluttering with every thrust. Soon the convulsions started at the base.

"God, Stacy. God!"

He thrust once more, and then he tensed as he filled the condom with his seed. He let out a ragged groan of release.

He pulled out and disposed of the condom quickly in the wastebasket next to the bed. How selfish could he be? He'd wanted to make her come again. She'd just lain there while he fucked her like a goddamned animal.

He lay back down next to her and swept a few strands of hair out of her eyes. "I'm sorry, Stace."

"For what? It felt wonderful."

He smiled. "I'm glad. But I wanted you to come again."

She let out a short giggle. "There's plenty of time for that, handsome."

"I'm afraid I need a few minutes." He raked his hand through his moist hair.

"Not a problem. We've got time." She sat up. "Are you hungry?"

On cue, his stomach growled. "Yeah. I could eat."

She reached for the phone on the nightstand. "I'm famished. Let's order some food."

Food? Okay, that would work. He needed to get to know this woman whose sexuality and beauty had ensnared him. One romp in the hay did not a relationship make, and a relationship was what he needed. A relationship that she couldn't do without. Somehow, he had to become irreplaceable to her. Fucking her without giving her another orgasm hadn't been a great start...

"What do you want?" he asked, grabbing the room service menu from the nightstand. "It's on me." Room service food was expensive, but this was an investment in his future.

"That's kind of you. But you don't have to—"

He took the phone from her and placed the receiver back on the cradle. "I insist. Let's see..." He perused the menu. "What sounds good? How about strawberries and champagne?" He grinned.

She answered with a smile. Then, "That sounds wonderful, but I'm craving something a little more...substantial."

"Strawberries dipped in chocolate?" he teased.

"The strawberries and champagne sound great. Just add a corned beef sandwich."

A woman who liked to eat. He could get behind that. His Italian Catholic mother loved to feed people, and he, an accomplished cook himself, had inherited her passion for the art. "I don't see a corned beef sandwich on the menu." He continued to glance over the options. "There's lasagna, though. You like Italian?"

"Love Italian."

He grinned. "Good girl. Of course, I really should only feed you the lasagna I make myself. I'm sure it's far superior to whatever slop they make here."

"This is a five star restaurant in a five star hotel," Stacy said, throwing a pillow at him.

"Let's just say I'm picky when it comes to Italian."

"Okay, no Italian then."

"I'll make you lasagna."

She let out a laugh. "How exactly do you plan to do that? Hijack the kitchen?"

"Well...not tonight, I guess. Sometime soon."

"Right." She grabbed the menu from him. "Let me look. I'll have...the club sandwich. That'll do fine. What do you want?" She picked up the phone.

"I'll have the same. But don't forget the strawberries and champagne. And charge it to room 311."

"Michael..."

"I said I insist."

"Okay," she relented. She ordered the food, replaced the phone on the cradle, and excused herself to go to the bathroom.

Now what? His cock stiffened. He could make love to her again, but they'd no doubt be interrupted by a knock on the door delivering the food.

He sat down in a nearby chair and leafed through a magazine until the whoosh of water met his ears. She was taking a shower? The image of water droplets trickling over that buxom body caused blood to rush to his groin. He imagined her arching her back, raking her fingers through her long wet hair. Massaging shampoo into her scalp and working it through to the ends, soap dropping from her hair onto her plump breasts, down her soft belly, into the curls between her legs...

Could he join her?

Should he?

The knock on the door saved him from the decision. After the waiter left, Michael popped open the champagne. The strawberries were displayed in a silver bowl with a glass of chocolate syrup in the middle. Perfect. He arranged the two club sandwiches on the table and set the strawberries in the middle. He poured two flutes of champagne and waited for Stacy.

When the water stopped running, his heart began to race.

Silly, he knew. He'd already had her, but all he could think about was having her again. He wanted to feed her strawberries, draw circles of chocolate around her luscious nipples and lick them. Chocolate, yes...chocolate on those amazing pussy lips of hers...

She came out of the bathroom clad in one of the hotel robes. Her hair was wet and combed back over her forehead, making her facial features prominent. Her big eyes seemed even bigger and browner, her lips fuller, redder, and perfectly sculpted. Her face was a perfect oval, her cheekbones high and chiseled.

Quite a beauty. He wondered briefly what had led to her divorce. What kind of idiot would let a gem like her go?

He shook his head to clear his thoughts. Developing feelings for Stacy Summers was *not* on the agenda. This was business, pure and simple.

"Hey, beautiful, the food's here."

"Sorry, I was feeling all sweaty."

"And that's a bad thing?"

She laughed. Her laugh was like a tinkling bell, cute and infectious. "Not a bad thing, handsome. I just want to be fresh for you."

"You look amazing."

"I look like I just got out of the shower. Not at my best, but clean."

"Well, I can't wait to dirty you up again. And that wasn't fair, by the way."

"What wasn't fair?" She squeezed a small amount of water from her hair.

"You taking a shower without me."

"Oh." She let out a nervous giggle. "I didn't actually decide to take a shower until I got into the bathroom. I looked in the mirror and I looked like such a mess, so I—"

"Are you kidding?" He stalked toward her and opened her robe. Her breasts beckoned. "You looked great. There's nothing sexier than a woman who's just been fucked." He took one breast in the palm of his hand. Heavy and plump, it fell in a beautiful mass, filling his hand perfectly. "I'll forgive you for leaving me out on one condition."

"What's that?" She smiled, and her lips trembled a little.

Was she nervous? After what they'd just shared? He squeezed the breast in his hand and ran his thumb over the tight nipple. "Next time you take a shower, you invite me. In fact"—he eyed the table, specifically the strawberries and chocolate—"I think I can guarantee you'll keep that promise."

"Oh? How's that?"

He sauntered to the table, picked up a strawberry, and swirled it in the chocolate. He returned to Stacy, who was still standing with her robe open, her lush breasts in full view. Michael grinned as he touched the chocolate-covered fruit to the tip of one pert nipple.

"I'll just get you dirty again."

★ ★ ★

Stacy shuddered. The sauce was warm, like hot fudge, and it seemed to light her nipple on fire. The intense heat surged through her and landed between her legs. Michael busied himself painting her other nipple, and as the sauce dripped down over her areolas, her breasts, and her belly, Stacy felt as though she were dripping to the floor as well. Fresh nectar gushed from her pussy and dripped down her thighs.

What was going on? Confusion coursed through her brain like a speeding bullet. Why was Michael Moretti doing this to her? What on earth did he see in Stacy Oppenheimer, introvert extraordinaire? The girl who walked into a room and was invisible?

Maybe she should lay it on the table and just ask him.

"Michael."

"Hmm?" He delicately traced her areola with the strawberry tip. Her robe slid off her shoulders and puddled to the floor. The chocolate was long gone now, and the friction from the tiny strawberry seeds tightened her sensitive skin even further.

"I...I don't understand."

"Don't understand what, baby?"

"What you're doing here."

"That's an easy one." He raised the strawberry to her lips and traced them.

Seemingly of its own accord, her tongue darted out and tasted the tang of fruit and the bittersweetness of chocolate.

"I'm painting you with chocolate. Then I'm going to lick it off you. And then I'm going to put you back in the shower, only I'm going with you this time."

"Oh, lord..." Stacy's head spun. Her wet tresses clung to her shoulders and back while her core heated. Really, did it matter why Michael Moretti was painting her with chocolate? Why he wanted to shower with her? Why he seemed to want to make love to her?

Correction—fuck her. This was not lovemaking. It was fucking, pure and simple.

Still, there were over one thousand women at this conference, all of whom would love the chance to spend an evening in Michael Moretti's arms. He could have any of them, and he had chosen her. Amazing.

Why question it? She might not like the answer.

She could like the experience, though. Indeed, she *did* like the experience. So far she liked it a lot. And she was comfortable—more comfortable than she thought possible with this handsome man who seemed to want her. Though not quite ready to completely shed her introvert status, she had stumbled way out of her comfort zone tonight.

It felt damn good.

"Baby?"

"Yeah?" She looked up at Michael who took a small bite of the strawberry.

"You ready for me to clean you up now?" He gave her a saucy grin.

The chocolate had cooled. What her flesh needed now was Michael's warm lips. "Oh, yes, I'm ready, Michael."

"Mmm, me too." He lowered his head and swirled his tongue around one nipple, licking the chocolate from her puckered skin. "Delicious." He snickered. "And the chocolate's not bad either."

Her cheeks warmed. His tongue was smooth compared to the dimpled fruit of the strawberry. And warm, oh so warm. Despite its warmth, shivers coursed through her. Her clit throbbed. Damn, why hadn't he painted her down there? Painted the lips of her pussy, the crease between her ass cheeks? Oh, to feel his slippery tongue there...

Her nipples hardened as he cleaned the other one and headed downward to the trails of chocolate that had dripped over her breasts and belly. His cock jutted outward. God, was it even larger than before? Large and beautiful and just waiting for...

"Michael..."

"What, beautiful?"

"Is there...more chocolate?"

"Of course, there's plenty. Your sandwich is here too."

Sandwich? Right, she'd been famished. She still was... though not for food at the moment. What she wanted now was one giant chocolate-covered cock.

She glanced over at the table where the food sat. A small silver bowl held the chocolate, surrounded by the strawberries in a larger bowl. She grabbed several strawberries and picked up the bowl of chocolate.

She turned toward Michael. "Get on the bed," she said, her voice an octave lower than normal.

He smiled and arched his eyebrows. "What do you have in mind, Stace?"

She winked at him. Winked! Stacy Oppenheimer winked at a man! Stopping the train of thought, she headed to the bathroom for a towel. No use soiling the sheets if the chocolate didn't stay put.

When she returned, Michael was lying on his back, his cock at attention, his grin saucy and wicked. "Got plans for me?"

"Oh, yes." She positioned the towel underneath him. "I just love chocolate, don't you?"

"I'd say I've already proved that."

She stared for a moment, fear threatening to paralyze her. Quickly, she channeled Starr again. She'd come this far, and she couldn't stop now. The few times she'd given David head had been failures in her mind. He hadn't said anything bad about it, though he hadn't said he enjoyed it either. God knew Michael had experience. He'd know she was a novice as soon as she touched her mouth to him.

Starr, I need you! Starr gave great head. All the men she slept with raved about her oral skills. Just pretend you're licking an ice cream cone, Starr often advised other women. It was a line Stacy had heard in a movie once. It worked for Starr, but Stacy *made* it work for Starr.

Would it actually work in reality?

No time like the present to find out. She'd have the chocolate to make the illusion even more real.

She knelt between Michael's muscular legs. Another part of him that was perfectly formed. They could have been sculpted by a Renaissance artist. Dark hair dusted the sinewy flesh. His balls hung under his penis, beckoning to be touched, licked.

"Wow," she said.

"Wow what?"

"Wow, you are one finely made man, Michael Moretti. But I'm sure you hear that all the time."

"It's never sounded sweeter than right now." He stroked his fingers through her damp hair. "And I mean that."

A line, of course. But a damned good one. She smiled and twirled the tip of a strawberry in the chocolate. "Such a finely made man should be painted, don't you think?"

"I'm game for whatever you have in mind, sweetheart."

"What I have in mind is to paint this beautiful shaft of yours and then lick every bit off you."

His thighs tensed around her head, and his balls bunched up slightly. Could her words be turning him on? A feeling of power surged into her. She actually had power over this stud of a man. How amazing!

She started at the base of his cock and drew the chocolate-covered fruit upward. Tiny shudders racked through him.

"Mmm. God, baby."

"Good?"

"Yeah it's good. Fuck!"

When she got to his cockhead, she swirled the strawberry around the tip and then gently poked it into the tiny opening.

"Fuck, baby!"

She smiled. Having a man at her mercy felt great! She reached forward and held the strawberry to his lips. He took a bite. She grabbed another one and began the torture again. When his penis was covered in delectable chocolate, she ate the last strawberry and prepared for the next phase in her plan.

Operation ice cream cone.

CHAPTER FIVE

Stacy inhaled a deep breath. Courage. She'd come this far, now for the *piece de resistance*. She closed her eyes and launched herself into one of Starr's infamous blow job scenes.

Eye contact. That was the first thing to remember during oral sex. She grasped Michael's cock and opened her eyes. His gaze was focused on her, his hazel eyes burning. He didn't smile. His lips were pulled taut and tense, as though he were waiting for something, which, of course, he was. Stacy lowered her lids just a touch, hoping she returned his smoldering stare. Still locking her gaze with his, she touched the tip of her tongue to his cockhead.

He visibly shuddered. How empowering! She touched his head again, with a bit more pressure this time. The warm chocolate slid over her tongue. Mmm, she did love chocolate, almost as much as she was growing to love her power over Michael Moretti's cock. She lapped at the head as though it were a scoop of dark chocolate ice cream sitting on top of a sugar cone, a swirl here, a lick there...until every bit of chocolate had been removed.

"God, Stace, that's amazing." Michael's voice was raspy, even a little jittery.

Power. She loved it.

She eased her mouth over the head of his cock and slid it downward, sucking the rest of the chocolate off his thick shaft.

His groan was her reward.

"Baby, that's so good, the way you suck me."

Up and down she moved, stifling her gag reflex as his tip hit the back of her throat. If she moved quickly, she found she could deep throat. A spike of pride jolted into her. Stacy Oppenheimer could deep throat Michael Moretti!

When her jaw needed a break, she trailed her lips down his shaft to his sack and rained tiny kisses over his balls. They bunched up as his thighs tensed around her head. She sucked one and then the other into her mouth, relishing his soft moans. Words met her ears—sexy words, endearing words, words telling her how hot she was, how much he loved what she was doing to him—words that made her pussy pulse with renewed energy and nectar.

This was turning her on.

His cock was glistening with her saliva. She slid her fist up and down his shaft as she continued to explore the peaks and valleys of his sack. She inhaled his musky odor, nibbled the soft skin of his inner thighs.

"Damn, you're good at this," Michael panted.

Good at this? If one was good at what one enjoyed, she was definitely good at sucking Michael's cock. She smiled against his balls and thrust her mouth onto his shaft once more, sucking more firmly.

"I'm going to come, Stace," he said. "God, I'm going to come."

Stacy widened her eyes, pierced his greenish gaze with her own. Could she handle him coming in her mouth?

Starr Shannon could.

So could Stacy Oppenheimer.

She sucked harder, cupping his balls, massaging them. With his groan came his seed. It gushed over her tongue and throat. She savored its slightly bitter flavor. This was a victory for Stacy the introvert, a victory to relish.

She let his cock drop from her lips and swallowed his essence. Still locking her gaze with his, she glided up his glistening body, letting her breasts press into his chest, and gave him a light kiss on the lips.

"Mmm, thank you," he said.

She let out a tiny laugh. "For what?"

He grinned. "What do you think?"

"That? Oh, that was my pleasure."

"And mine." He snuggled her against his body and kissed the top of her head.

Stacy was ripe for more, but fatigue had its own idea. As she cuddled into Michael and his breathing turned shallow, she drifted into peaceful slumber.

Stacy jerked upright. A strange sound buzzed in her ears. The covers next to her were rumpled. Where was Michael? Had he left?

Well, so what if he had? He certainly didn't owe her anything. This had been a fuck for him, nothing more. She had known that going in.

Still, her heart danced a two-step when he sauntered out of the bathroom, naked and glorious. He hadn't left her.

"Hey, beautiful," he said, smiling. "Ready for that shower you owe me?"

The whoosh of the shower. That was the strange sound. Not so strange now. A shower with Michael Moretti. Had she died and gone to heaven?

She stood, suddenly shy again, and draped the sheet around her body.

"Oh, no." He walked toward her. "No covering up that work of art." He tugged at a corner of the sheet, and it fell into a rumpled puddle at her feet.

Stacy grimaced. Her hair had to be a mass of red-brown tangles. She had fallen asleep while it was wet. Lord, and he was calling her a work of art?

"Michael, I need to brush out my hair, and go to the bathroom. Can you...?"

"Nope. Not leaving, Stace. I'm getting in that shower with you come hell or high water."

"Geez..."

"What's wrong? I've seen every inch of you, and I adore every inch of you." He traced her jawline with long finger. "You're gorgeous."

Her belly flip-flopped. He sure sounded sincere. Whether it was an act or not, why not live the fantasy a little longer? "Okay. Give me a minute. I'll meet you in the shower."

She hightailed it into the bathroom, ran a brush through her hair—which was every bit the mess she'd thought it was—and took care of necessary business.

"Ready, Michael," she called, and she stepped into the steaming shower.

The raining water soothed her skin. She closed her eyes and arched her back, letting her hair flow down her back in a silky mass.

"Now that's a lovely sight."

His voice was a growling sigh, and Stacy opened her eyes to Michael's perfect physique. She smiled. "Hi."

"Hi, yourself." He grabbed a bar of soap and lathered it

between his palms. "May I?"

She nodded. His masculine hands smoothed the lather over her shoulders, over the hills of her breasts, over her taut belly. Her nipples hardened at his touch.

"I need some soap too," he said. "Come here."

He pulled her into his body, and she rubbed her breasts against his muscled torso. His black chest hair tickled her nipples, and she couldn't help the small sigh that escaped her throat. So hard and masculine, he was, and so handsome and sexy. She pressed her cheek against his beefy shoulder and closed her eyes. Smooth strokes caressed her back, glided downward over the globes of her ass cheeks, slid between her legs. Her mound sprang to life.

"Hmm. You wet from the shower?" Michael teased, "or for me?"

She grinned into his hard shoulder. "For you, of course."

"Then we need to do something about that. Luckily, I came prepared." He picked up a condom from the soapdish. "Now, kiss me."

His lips crushed to hers.

The kiss was anything but gentle. He forced her lips open and thrust his tongue inside. His groan vibrated against the inside of her mouth. It was a hungry kiss, a kiss of the passion that sizzled between them.

Stacy opened to him, let her tongue duel with his. His hands coasted down her arms, and the faint ripple of a foil packet breached the haze of her thoughts.

"Turn around, baby."

She obeyed, and he gripped her hips and slowly slid into her. Lord, what a sweet invasion! Ripe and juicy, her slick passage welcomed him.

Slowly, gently, so unlike the kiss they had just shared, he made love to her.

"You feel so good, Stace." He pistoned his hips, caressed her ass. "So good."

"Yes, so good," she echoed.

One strong hand slid over her hip, fingers entwined in her nest of curls and found her hard nub. He rubbed it in smooth circles, in time with his rhythmic thrusts into her, and the crescendo built.

Stacy closed her eyes, savored the warm rain on her face, her shoulders, her breasts.

Talented hands played her clit, the pressure growing, ascending, until a curtain opened over the last vestiges of her control. Michael pumped and pumped, rocking her hips.

"Yes, yes!" The dam burst, and her body shook. Her wet hands slipped from their grip on the shower wall, but Michael steadied her, continued to plunge into her as her whole torso seemed to spasm around him. Silver sparks shot through her arms and legs, yet still he held her stable, his strength her protective fort.

"That's it, baby." He rocked in time with the euphoric convulsions inside her. "Make it last. Come for me."

Again and again her body imploded upon itself, her skin alternately heated and cooled. The warm rain from the shower intensified the sensations, and the heady splashes of water accompanied each thrust of Michael's cock.

"Yeah, baby, that's it," he said again. "God, baby, I'm going to come!"

His thrusts quickened, and he let out a groan as he plunged even farther into her. His contractions pounded against her sensitive walls, and her heart sped with the knowledge that he was feeling what she was feeling—wild, free, and sexual.

His chin poked into her shoulder, and his breath blew the droplets from her neck. Still the water pelted them, and still their bodies were joined. They stood for a few timeless moments, and peace—pure peace—blanketed Stacy's body and mind.

"That was wonderful." Michael's voice brought reality.

"Yes, it was," she agreed.

Michael withdrew and turned Stacy to face him. He threaded his fingers through her sopping hair. "I love your hair," he said. "Could I wash it?"

Wash her hair? What a turn on. She wasn't sure why, but the thought of those strong hands on her scalp enthralled her. "Sure. If I can wash yours."

"Deal." He smiled and picked up the small bottle of hotel shampoo in the corner of the shower. He lathered some in his palm and spread it over Stacy's head.

Since when had shampooing become such an erotic art? Michael's fingers worked magic on her head. She closed her eyes and enjoyed. When he thought he got soap in her eye, he apologized profusely. She laughed and told him not to worry, that she was fine. He continued his massage, and when he finished, he tilted her head back and rinsed her, threading the soap through the ends of her hair until it all disappeared down the drain.

She traded places with him and squirted a quarter-size puddle of shampoo into her palm. His hair hung in dark waves and clung to his cheeks and neck. Gorgeous thick Italian hair, and she couldn't wait to work her fingers into it. It was as soft and silky as she'd imagined, and she gently scrubbed his tresses and worked the soap through the ends.

Like her, he shut his eyes and leaned back. He was so tall she had to reach to get the top of his scalp, but she stretched gladly, wanting to give him the same attention he'd given her.

"Okay, you can rinse now," she said.

He turned into the water, and she helped him work the lather out of his hair. When they were both soap free, he took her into his arms and stared into her eyes, his own smoldering.

She caressed the corded muscle of his neck, the sinew of his bulging biceps, and the strong lines of his back. His mouth lowered, as if in slow motion, until his lips touched hers.

Though it lacked the fervency and possessiveness of their earlier kisses, it was beautiful. It was timeless.

Emotion as thick as the steam surrounded her.

God!

She pulled away.

What had she done? Emotion had no place here. This was an affair. No, not even an affair. A fuck. A one-night stand.

"What's wrong?" Michael's hazel eyes widened.

Good lord, he was gorgeous, his now-clean hair slicked back on his head, his perfect face dripping with water.

Stacy turned off the faucet. "Time to get out. I'm wrinkled as a prune."

"A beautiful prune."

Without responding, she stepped out of the shower, wrapped herself in a towel, and threw one to him.

"Thanks." He wrapped the towel around his waist.

Why did he have to look like a Greek god? Or an Italian god? The stark white of the towel contrasted with his olive skin. So beautiful.

He grabbed another towel and started rubbing his hair. "Why so quick to get out?"

Stacy cleared her throat. "No reason. Other than I have a conference to attend today. I'm sure I've already missed the first few workshops. I have no idea what time it is."

"I don't either." He grinned. "And I don't care."

"Well, I do. This is my business."

"It's my business too, remember?" He launched the towel he'd used on his hair onto the shower rim. "Is there anywhere you absolutely have to be today?"

"Well, I have a book signing tomorrow, but today, no. I'm not required to be anywhere. But I should—"

He touched his fingers to her lips. "I have two photo shoots tomorrow, but I'm free as a bird today. So I have a suggestion."

Her lips tingled from his soft touch. With a shiver, she said, "What?"

"Take the day off. Play hooky with me."

"Hooky?" What was he? Fifteen?

He laughed. "Yeah. Hooky. Let's be immature for the day. There's something I'd love to share with you. One of my favorite things in the world."

"Oh?" Her curiosity was piqued. "What's that?"

"Sky diving."

CHAPTER SIX

"Are you out of your fucking mind?"

Sky diving? Stacy Oppenheimer, classic introvert, might have given a male model some killer head, but jumping out of an airplane was out of the question.

"It's a hobby of mine. I'd like to take you."

Stacy shook her head. "So not happening, Michael."

"I'm a qualified instructor."

"Don't care."

"All I need to do is call my friend Oliver who owns the plane and equipment. He'll take us up today."

"What if he's already booked?"

"He's not."

"Right. How do you know?"

He winked. "I already booked him for today."

"God." Stacy rolled her eyes. "So you were planning to skip out of the conference today anyway."

"Yes, I was. Still am. Having you accompany me will make it all the better."

"Well, you have a jolly time. I'll just be here, attending workshops. On the ground."

"Oh, come on, Stace. Live a little."

Live a little? She'd spent the night making love to a cover model. She'd had two orgasms, a first for her. Hadn't she done enough living? For this week, anyway?

"Thanks, but no thanks."

"But I want to spend the day with you."

"Then stay here at the conference. That's where I'll be."

"I'll make it worth your while..." His tone was teasing.

How could he possibly give her more than he already had? "Just exactly how do you plan to do that?"

"Well..." He stalked toward her, loosened her towel, and let it drop to the floor. "I could lavish these remarkable breasts with some more attention." He cupped them and circled his thumbs over her nipples. "Or I could lick that sweet pussy of yours for a couple of hours. That would be a true pleasure for you *and* for me."

"Michael, you're an incredible lover." At least he was as far as she knew in her limited experience. "But I'll be honest with you. Skydiving scares the shit out of me."

He smirked. "Are you a woman or an amoeba?"

Though embarrassment flooded her that he'd remembered that stupid line, she couldn't help but laugh. "You're throwing that back at me?"

He joined in her laughter. "It seemed to fit."

She shook her head. "Michael, I don't understand you."

"What's not to understand? I just spent the night with a beautiful lady. I'd like to spend the day with her too."

Could this be more than a one-night stand? A two night stand maybe? Or at least a night and a day stand? "But sky diving?"

"Tell you what"—he kissed her ear—"I will personally guarantee your safety. I want to make sure you get back in one piece to all those who care about you."

Stacy snorted. Who? No one cared about her. "There's no one to get back to, Michael. You know I'm divorced and I never had kids. Both my parents are dead, and I don't have any brothers and sisters."

"Geez, Stace, I'm sorry."

"Don't be sorry. I'm fine with it. But frankly, no one would notice if I was gone."

He smiled. "I would. In fact, I'll guarantee you that it will be the best experience of your life." He bit her lobe. "Excluding last night, of course."

Tingles skittered over her skin. Why did his touch affect her so?

"Come on, Stace. What is it? Are you afraid of heights?"

"No, it's nothing like that." *Just afraid of my own shadow.* But admittedly, she'd come a long way in the past twenty-four hours. Starr would sky dive. Could Stacy?

"Then live a little."

She plunked her head on his broad shoulder. "Okay," she said timidly.

"What was that? Say it again."

She lifted her head and punched him in the arm. "You heard me. Geez, Michael. I can't believe I'm going to do this."

"I promise you'll love it." He brushed his lips against hers.

★ ★ ★

"I think I'm going to throw up."

Michael adjusted the hooks on Stacy's gear. He spoke loudly over the aircraft engine. "You'll be fine, Stace."

She tried to soothe her stomach by breathing deeply. The sporadic lunges of the small aircraft weren't helping her cause. How could practicing jumping out of a plane and studying free fall maneuvers and parachute deployment for only an hour prepare her for this?

"What if the chute doesn't open?"

"I'll take care of the chute. You let me worry about that."

She and Michael would be tandem skydiving, which was the best method, he had explained, for the first jump. Rather than jumping on her own, she'd be harnessed to Michael, her qualified instructor—help!—who would be responsible for safe and timely deployment of the parachute. This method freed Stacy to concentrate on freefall, piloting the canopy, and landing.

Yeah, right.

Like she'd remember anything about piloting a canopy when she was plummeting to the earth at a gazillion miles per hour.

"You've secured the extra parachute, right?" she said loudly but timidly.

"Yes, baby. It's all secure."

"'Kay." Her heart slammed into her sternum. Why was she doing this again?

"We're going to be strapped together, your back to my front. That's kind of a turn on, don't you think?" Michael's low voice carried across the noise.

"Michael, if you wanted to be strapped to me, we don't have to jump out of a plane to do it."

His buoyant laugh filled the small aircraft. "I'll hold you to that. *After* our jump." He tightened another buckle. "You're all secure, Stace. Now, let me just hook us together, okay?"

"No hurry."

The loud roar of the small aircraft engine buzzed in her ear. *Calm down*, she told herself. *You're an intelligent woman. You know what to do. And Michael's an experienced sky diver...* Just words. Words that weren't helping her nerves one bit.

"We're about ready, Oliver!" Michael yelled to the pilot.

The small plane swerved. Stacy nearly lost her balance, but Michael's arms steadied her as he fastened the straps of their equipment together.

"We just hit 13,000 feet!" Oliver's voice rumbled from the cockpit.

"Perfect!" Michael said. "It's a great day, too. So clear and warm."

Yeah, just perfect. Perfectly nauseating. Stacy's stomach churned. "Michael," she said shakily. "I can't do this. I just can't."

"You'll be fine, beautiful."

His breath caressed her neck. And was that his erection? Couldn't be, not through all their gear.

"I promise you'll be fine."

A jolt of turbulence hit the plane, and Stacy's feet nearly left the floor of the aircraft.

"I promise our ride will be smoother than this," Michael said. "Ready?"

Stacy squeezed her eyes shut and took a deep breath. "What if I can't steer?"

"Don't worry about that. I'll steer, okay? You just enjoy yourself. Ready now?"

"Ready as I'll ever be."

"Okay, baby." He edged her to the opening. "Let's go."

Once airborne, Stacy couldn't remember Michael's exit count or actually leaving the plane. For a moment, she had the feeling of jetting forward as well as down. Michael had told her about that. Physics. It was the momentum created by the plane's speed. The "forward throw" he had called it. She was surprised she remembered.

He'd also explained that she wouldn't feel like she was falling, but no words had prepared her for the buoyancy that enveloped her. Was she truly dropping? The ground didn't seem to be getting any nearer. Free fall is what Michael called this portion of the jump. A rush of adrenaline hit her gut, spiked through her like a massive dose of endorphins. The sensation resembled floating in water, yet was more pure, less dense. Freedom. Total freedom. She was truly flying. Flying in Michael's arms. The feeling of security surprised her, and she savored it, letting herself take in the beauty of the sky and the earth so far below. Wisps of clouds whirled around her head. The crisp azure of the heavens, so beautiful in their totality.

Too soon, Michael yelled that he was releasing the chute.

Steering. She should be steering. She tensed.

Michael must have sensed her unease, because he shouted, "Just enjoy yourself. I've got the canopy!"

So enjoy herself she did.

She'd thought she'd been flying before. No, that had been mere floating. Now, she and Michael jutted forward at what seemed like a ferocious speed. This part of the jump would last about five minutes, Michael had said.

Stacy's heart soared! Her mind buzzed. Why had she been so scared? Suddenly, she envied birds their wings. If only she could feel this free, this content, always.

God... Her stomach rolled. Now, the ground was approaching. Why hadn't she noticed how close they were before?

"It's okay, baby, we're doing fine," Michael assured her.

They landed with a jolt. Stacy's heart dropped to her feet. Michael steadied her, managed to kiss her neck despite all the gear between them. The chute floated around them in a rippling haze.

Quickly, Michael unbuckled them, and Stacy turned and threw her arms around him. Their safety goggles clinked, their straps scraped, but Stacy didn't care.

So many words clogged her throat. She wanted to tell him what the jump had meant to her, how it had freed a part of her that had been long imprisoned. How it had broken the rest of the shell around her spirit, the shell that he'd already cracked with his wonderful lovemaking and her first orgasm. She wanted to describe the euphoria she'd felt while free falling, the rush of the forward throw. Mostly she wanted to tell him what he had come to mean to her in so short a time.

Those three scary words formed in her mouth.

But no words emerged. Her emotion was too thick, too buoyant for speech.

She simply wrapped herself as close as she could to the man she'd come to adore.

★ ★ ★

"You wouldn't believe it," Stacy said to Veronica at dinner. Michael and Dino also sat at their table for four. "You've got to try it, Ronnie. I swear, you'll be hooked!"

"Jump out of a plane?" The younger woman shook her head. "No thanks. I like my feet planted firmly on the ground."

"You'd love it," Michael said. "If I could convince Stace to go, I can convince anyone."

"Sure enough," Dino agreed. "It's an amazing experience. I've only done it once, but it was a feeling I'll never forget."

"Well, maybe I'll let you convince me sometime," Veronica laughed. "I'm heading to the moonlight erotic readings. Any of you want to come along?"

Dino grinned. "I'm game. You guys in?"

Michael shook his head. "I want to dance." He stood and held out his hand to Stacy. "May I?"

She smiled. He looked so regal in his tux. All the cover models were dressed formally for tonight's dinner. They'd been on duty during the meal itself, but now that dessert was over, they were free for the evening. Michael and Dino had gravitated toward Stacy and Veronica.

Dino shared some of Michael's sultry Italian features, but though Dino was a handsome man, there was no comparison in Stacy's mind. Michael was the best looking man at the conference and on the planet.

"I'd love to dance, thanks," she said. "But will you excuse me for a minute? I need to make a phone call."

"Sure." He brushed his lips against her cheek. "Don't be long."

Stacy left the ballroom, made a quick phone call to her neighbor to check on her cat, and then headed toward the bathroom to check her makeup.

As she walked through the hallway, Veronica's voice rang out from one of the workshop rooms. Not one to eavesdrop, Stacy kept walking but stopped when she heard her name.

"...do that to Stacy."

Do what to Stacy? Stacy stood near enough to hear as best she could through the semi-open door but far enough against the wall of the hallway so as not to be seen.

"His plan..." Dino's words trailed off.

What plan. Was he talking about Michael? For a moment she wished for one of those ear phone things on late night television that allowed a person to overhear conversations.

"That's horrible!"

Veronica's shrill outrage was easy to hear.

"I'm not saying I agree," Dino said. Then, unintelligible mumblings.

"Sugar mama?" Veronica again. "He did *not* use that term!"

"He did. He knows his career.... He wants to....the way he's been living."

Stacy tried furiously to decipher Dino's meaning, until Veronica's voice carried right outside into the hallway.

"Stacy doesn't have any money!"

"Bestselling author... Grandmother...."

Stacy's heart dropped to her belly. Money? Michael thought she had money? She made a decent living, but she was hardly rolling in it. She was a bestselling author, yes. A bestselling erotic e-book author. Hardly the bigtime. She was lucky enough not to work a day job, but wealthy she was not. She lived in a two bedroom townhome with her cat. She had a car payment and a mortgage and some months, when royalties were low, she ate a lot of hamburger and ramen noodles.

Had Michael been playing her? The sky diving, the lovemaking—had it all been a ploy to ingratiate himself to her so she'd take care of him? He wanted to be her "kept man?"

"Well, I'm not going to let him do that to Stacy."

Veronica stormed out of the room, her full lips in a taut line.

"Ronnie, wait! You can't tell him I told you—"

Dino ran out the door after her. They both stopped short when they saw Stacy.

"Oh, Stace. Oh, God," Veronica said.

"You don't have to tell him anything, Ronnie," Stacy said.

"I've heard enough already, and I'll tell him myself."

Emotion stormed through Stacy as she ran to the elevator and hit fifteen. No! No, damn it! Why did this have to happen? God, she'd let herself fall in love with the bastard!

Tears streamed down her cheeks. Was she sad? Angry? So many different feelings gripped her insides, surged through her veins. Finally, when the elevator dinged her arrival, one sensation stood out among the others.

Betrayal.

Though the bed had been made and no longer showed the remnants of their lovemaking, Michael's suitcase sat at the edge of the wardrobe. Her own fault, of course. After their amazing afternoon, she'd invited him to move into her room for the remainder of the conference.

Well, he could now consider himself uninvited.

Not satisfied to merely push the suitcase out into the hallway, she opened it. Inside sat his underwear, his sundries, his shirts and jeans. One by one, she pulled them out and tossed them into the hallway as she sobbed incoherently.

"How could you, you fucking asshole?"

Boxer briefs, jeans, tight T-shirts littered the hallway. In the bottom of his suitcase was a cobalt bottle of vodka. "Yeah. I suppose you thought you'd get me drunk. Well, I'd have to be drunk to sleep with you again." She threw the bottle into the hallway where it smashed into icy blue shards against the wall.

Last, she threw the empty suitcase into the hallway amidst the designer clothes, the expensive cologne, the razor, the toothpaste and toothbrush...

She slammed her door shut, flung herself on her bed, and wept some more.

CHAPTER SEVEN

Oh shit.

Clearly, this wasn't leading to anything good. Michael shuffled through his belongings cluttering the hallway outside Stacy's room. He should call housekeeping to clear away the glass from the broken bottle of vodka, but first, he needed to see Stacy and make sure she was all right. His skin tightened. Fuck. He was actually nervous.

What had gone wrong? Thank God she'd given him her extra keycard. He slid it into the lock and opened the door.

Darkness flooded the room. He switched on the light. Stacy was on the bed lying on her back, still in her scarlet formal gown, one arm flung over her eyes.

His heart thumped. "Stace?"

"Go away, Michael," she said without moving.

"Are you okay? Why are my things in the hallway?"

She snorted. "As if you don't know."

"I *don't* know, Stace. What's going on?"

"Get out."

"Not until you tell me you're okay."

"I'm fine. Now, get out."

He inched toward the bed. "Please, baby. Tell me what's wrong."

"Ask Dino and Ronnie. They'll tell you."

"I haven't seen Dino and Ronnie. You didn't come back for our dance, and I started to get worried. So I went looking for you."

"Too bad you didn't find Dino and Ronnie."

"I don't give a flying fuck about Dino and Ronnie right now, damn it! I only care about you!"

She scoffed. "Right."

His heart burst with sensation he couldn't describe. Worry. Intense longing. Sadness. What the hell was happening to him?

"Stace..."

"Get out, Michael."

"Won't you talk to me? Come on. You owe me that much."

She sat upright, her big baby browns afire. "Owe you? I don't owe you a goddamned thing, Michael Moretti. If there's one thing I'm certain of, it's *that*."

"But we shared—"

"We shared a fuck, Michael. A fuck. I knew what it was from the beginning. Don't think I didn't. I knew you didn't want me for me. I'm not an idiot, for God's sake."

"I did want you. I swear—"

"Shut up! Just shut the fuck up. I can't stand to listen to any more of your lies."

"Lies? I never lied to you, Stacy. I swear."

"God, you sling such bullshit. Do you ever listen to yourself?"

"I—"

"Too bad you didn't run into Dino and Ronnie. They'd have clued you in. Let's just say I stumbled into a very interesting conversation between your roomie and his current squeeze—and Ronnie deserves better, by the way."

Oh, God. Michael's insides squirmed. He had a feeling he knew where this was going. He'd told Dino... *Oh fuck.*

Why did it matter? Women like Stacy were a dime a

dozen, right? One rich older woman would give way to another, and then another, all too happy to pay for the privilege of his companionship.

Right?

Isn't that how it was supposed to work?

So why did it matter? So he'd invested twenty-four hours in Stacy Summers. Sure, she was easy on the eyes. Very easy. Damned good in bed too. But there were others just as easy on the eyes, just as good in bed, probably some with more money even. Chalk it up to experience and take the loss. Try again tomorrow. Tomorrow's another day and all that.

But Stacy... Fuck. He liked her. He really liked her. Liked fucking her. Liked sky diving with her. Hell, he liked *talking* to her. Who'd have thought?

"Listen, Stacy, I don't know what Dino told you—"

"He didn't tell me anything. He didn't have to tell me anything. I just got a clue, that's all. I'm a smart girl. You don't have to draw me a picture."

"So he didn't tell you about—"

"Hello? Are you listening? He didn't tell me anything. He told Ronnie, and I overheard it. Now, get out. I'm not anyone's sugar mama."

Fuck. "God, Stace. I'm sorry you had to hear that."

"So am I." She lay back down. "No, I'm not. I'm glad I know. I'm glad I know who you really are. What kind of man you really are. To think, I almost..."

"Almost what?"

"Never mind. Get out, Michael."

"Stace. Please. Can't we talk about this?"

"Talk about what? Are you going to deny what Dino said."

"Dino has a big mouth."

"I'm thankful he does."

"Yeah. Well, he'll hear from me. But Stace, I..." Words hung on his tongue, caught between mind and voice. He wasn't quite sure how to vocalize them.

"Good bye, Michael."

"What about our day together? Hell, what about our night together?"

"It was a fun romp. Now, it's over. *Ciao*."

"Can't we—"

She sat up again and reached for the phone. "No, we can't. Now leave, or I'll have you removed."

Michael exhaled. He knew when he'd been beaten. He just never expected to take anything this hard. Where were these feelings coming from?

He turned, walked toward the door, and opened it. He didn't look back.

That it took so much effort not to surprised him.

★ ★ ★

"Thanks a lot, pal."

Dino took a swig of his beer. "Hey, Ronnie and I tried to find you. I managed to do some damage control with her, but—"

"But nothing. Why didn't either of you go after Stacy?"

"Why would we? I mean, it's not like—"

"Damn it, Dino, I thought we were friends."

"Hell, Mike, you never said it was a secret."

"You really do have a brain the size of a pea, don't you?" Michael shook his head. "Does it take a genius to know you don't go telling a woman's friend what your friend has in mind for her friend?"

"Well, get a load of that. You actually have feelings for the woman."

"You're full of it. I loved a woman once. It's not worth the heartache."

"You can't always control your feelings, Michael. Even a pea brain like me knows that. Maybe you didn't mean to develop feelings for Stacy, but you did all the same."

"Shut the fuck up."

"If you didn't have feelings, you wouldn't be so upset about this."

He shook his head. "Yes, I have feelings. Feelings of the loss of twenty-four hours of this conference. Did it ever occur to you that maybe I don't want to start the whole process over? I invested a lot of time here. Maybe I found the woman I wanted, and now you fucked it up."

"There're a million women just as hot with just as much money who'd be glad to..."

Michael stopped listening. Yeah, he knew the drill. He'd gone through it in his own mind a thousand times since he'd left Stacy lying in bed, since he'd packed up his belongings in the hallway, since he'd picked up the blue glass from the broken vodka bottle. Yup, a million women. The thought should appease him.

It didn't, which mystified him.

"I told Ronnie. She understood. Said she'd talk to Stacy."

Dino's words sliced through the fog in Michael's brain. "Told Ronnie what?"

"About Beth. She nearly cried. She—"

"For God's sake!" Michael resisted the urge to pull his own hair out. "What the fuck did I ever do to you?"

"I was trying to control the damage! Fuck. I thought you'd appreciate—"

"Appreciate you spilling my life story to a complete stranger? Jesus Christ, Dino."

Michael seethed. Anger boiled inside him. Anger at Dino. Anger at Stacy for not listening to him. Anger at Beth for abandoning him all those years ago...

"I have to get out of here," he said, his blood boiling. "I need a drink. Or a smoke. Or something. God damn it! Anything!" His emotions rocked, threatened to spill into something unnameable. Something he couldn't fathom. His father. His asshole father....

He couldn't stay here. Couldn't go to Stacy for the comfort he craved in her arms.

Where to go?

Where?

He slammed the door.

★ ★ ★

Stacy pasted a smile on her face as she signed another book. These were her fans, the people who supported her, fed her, clothed her. She adored every one of them, and by God, she'd act her part today if it killed her. None of them would know her heart had been shattered into a billion tiny fragments.

"Thank you so much," the gushing woman said, taking her book. "I just love your work. Starr Shannon is one of my favorite characters."

"Thank you," Stacy said. "It means so much to a writer when a person enjoys her work."

"Could I ask you a question?"

Stacy nodded. "Of course."

"Have you ever considered making Starr a cougar?"

"A cougar?"

"Yeah, you know, give her a lover who's significantly younger? Like seven years or more?"

A cougar? Seven years or more? Michael was thirty-six to her forty-five. Did that make her—Stacy—a cougar?

Of course not, because they weren't in a relationship. They'd never been in a relationship. A one-night fuck did not a cougar make.

"I just always thought of Starr as the perfect cougar," the fan went on. "She's so sure of herself and so vibrant. I think a younger man would find her extremely sexy, and think of all she could teach him in the bedroom!"

Stacy let out a high-pitched laugh. Ha! A cougar teaching her younger man. A cub, isn't that what the younger lover was called? Heck, she hadn't taught Michael a thing. He'd taught *her*. Given her her first orgasm, no less.

But Starr... Starr could be a worthy instructor.

"Thank you"—she glanced at the woman's name tag— "Mary. I think that's a great idea. Starr would make a wonderful cougar."

"I'm so glad you think so!"

"In fact, when I write her cougar story, I'll dedicate it to you, how about that?"

"Oh my!" Mary nearly jumped out of her jeans. "That would be amazing!"

"Do you have a card?"

"No. I'm not an author, just a reader. I love these conferences."

"Here then." Stacy handed Mary one of her business

cards. "Write down your full name and your email address, and I'll be in touch."

Mary hastily jotted down her information and handed the card back to Stacy.

"Thanks, Mary." She gestured to the freebies on her table. "Don't forget to take some book marks and other goodies, okay? Thanks so much for stopping by."

"Not a problem," Mary gushed. "Not a problem at all!"

As Mary left the table, her hands full of Stacy's bookmarks, Stacy took a long drink from her bottle of water. She checked her watch. One more hour of book signing. One more hour. Her bags were packed and waiting at the front desk. Once the book signing was over, she was off to the airport to catch the next flight home on standby. She wasn't waiting until tomorrow.

She just couldn't.

She took another sip of water and swiped her hand across her brow. Damn, it was hot in here! It wouldn't hurt to get up for a few minutes. Take a quick walk to see if she could cool off. If nothing else, she could splash some cool water on her face in the restroom.

She stood and hurried away before anyone else came to her table. Once in the bathroom, she turned on the faucet and filled her palms with the cool liquid. She splashed it on her face and then regarded her reflection. Her eyes were still puffy from all the crying last night.

Well, nothing could be done about that. The cool water would help, at least.

She splashed her face again and then once more still before turning off the faucet and drying her skin gently with a paper towel.

Eyes were still a bit swollen, but at least her cheeks were

rosy and healthy looking. She quickly took a lipstick out of her handbag and applied it.

Not too bad, she thought, and headed back to the book signing.

Just as she was about to turn the corner to head into the ballroom where the signing was held, someone gripped her shoulder.

She jumped and soon found herself backed against the wall.

"It's just me, Stace."

That voice. That voice that had moaned her name.

"We need to talk, baby."

CHAPTER EIGHT

"We have nothing to talk about. I'm in the middle of a book signing." Stacy started forward, but Michael held her, wouldn't let her go.

"You have to listen to me. I—"

Stacy seethed, gathered all her strength, and pushed against his chest as hard as she could. "The only thing I have to do is get back to my signing!"

Michael didn't budge. Geez, he really was one solid mass of muscle.

"Have you talked to Ronnie?"

What the hell was he talking about? "Ronnie? I haven't seen her since last night. What does she have to do with anything?"

"Thank God." Michael's face softened a bit. His hazel eyes scorched her skin. "You look beautiful."

Now she knew he was full of it. She'd just seen her puffy brown eyes in the bathroom mirror. "Thanks. I'd like to think you mean that, but you're a known liar."

"I never lied to you."

"Right." She scoffed. "Let's just call it omission then. You neglected to tell me you were looking for a sugar mama."

"Look, I know you overheard Ronnie and Dino talking, but Dino didn't know what he was talking about. I swear it."

"Let me go, damn it!"

"No! Not until you listen to me!"

"I could listen all day, Michael, but I'll never believe a word you say."

"Oh?" His eyes burned, his nostrils flared. Ruddiness colored his chiseled olive cheeks. "Then maybe you'll believe this!"

His lips came down on hers with the force of a hurricane. Strong hands clamped her cheeks.

Stacy squirmed, pressed her lips together, tried, tried so hard...but it was too much. His mouth, though uninvited, was magic on hers. His kiss was hard, raw, and unapologetic, and it ignited fire in her veins. He hadn't shaved, and his rough stubble burned the soft skin of her cheeks. And that burning was good, so good. It added to the carnal intensity of their mouths mashing together. They ate at each other as though they'd been hungry for weeks. He plunged his fists into her hair, growled into her mouth.

They kissed and kissed, until Michael pulled away and drew a ragged breath. "Come with me."

He grabbed Stacy's hand and whisked her down the hallway to a secluded alcove.

"Michael, the booksign—"

"Fuck the book signing," he said, his voice a primitive snarl. He lifted her skirt and ripped off her lacy thong with his bare hands.

"Michael!"

"I need you, Stace. And by God, I'm going to have you. Now."

Stacy shuddered. She should run. Run screaming. But something in his voice, in his eyes, held her still. He wouldn't hurt her, she knew. Need burst to life in her core and rushed through her body. Juice trickled from her pussy.

Michael's fingers sought her slit. "God, you're wet. I knew you'd be wet for me."

Stacy closed her eyes and inhaled. If he didn't fuck her soon, she was sure she'd die an untimely death right here in the hotel hallway. The clink of his belt buckle and zing of his zipper buzzed in her ears. Then, the rip of the condom packet. He pushed her against the wall, lifted her, and set her down upon his cock.

Her body arched and her thighs opened. How glorious he felt inside her! She wrapped her thighs around his waist, hugged herself to him. She dug her nails into his shoulders and rocked upward, eagerly meeting every one of his thrusts.

"God, yeah, baby, that's it. Let me fuck you."

She leaned down and bit into the corded muscle of his neck. A salty tang danced across her tongue. She bit him again, wanting to mark him. To mark Michael Moretti as the property of Stacy Oppenheimer. She bit once more, harder still, and he rocketed into her with a growling gasp. A scraping at her neck made her wince. He was biting her, marking her too. Fuck, it was sexy.

Perspiration from their faces comingled, drizzling down their cheeks and necks. Stacy's breath came rapidly, her pulse racing, as she rode him with abandon. Tingles shot through her, and within moments, the familiar sparks jolted through her clit. God, she was coming, and oh, it was a good one!

"Michael!" Her voice sounded as though it were outside her body. "I'm coming!"

"Yeah, baby, come for me," he huffed.

She shot upward, coming down upon his cock just as she burst.

"Aaauugh!" He thrust harder. "God, I'm coming too!"

They rocked together, sharing the orgasm, until the electricity between them was so thick Stacy swore it was almost visible. Silvery threads joining them, joining their souls.

When the sparks settled, Stacy's head was on the moist hardness of Michael's shoulder. She raised it, looked around. Thank God the coast was clear. She eased herself downward, unclamping her legs from around Michael's hips. Her legs wobbled a little when her feet hit the ground, but she steadied herself and lowered her skirt. Her underwear was a lost cause.

She didn't look in his eyes. She couldn't. She feared what she might see and what he might see in hers. This wasn't just sex to her anymore, but it could never be what she wanted. He didn't want her. He wanted only a caretaker, a provider.

She said nothing as she pushed him away from her body.

"Stace?"

She looked at her watch. "I missed the end of the book signing."

"I'm sorry."

"No, you're not. But it doesn't matter. I'm leaving."

"What about us?"

"There is no us, Michael. There never was."

"But we just—"

"We just fucked, Michael." Stacy adjusted her skirt once more. "You're a fabulous fuck. I'll give you that. Whoever you end up with won't have any complaints."

She walked away.

He didn't follow her, and her disappointment that he didn't irked her. She'd been one last fuck to him. Silently, she berated herself for giving herself to him one last time. She'd been weak, but no longer.

After a quick trip to the restroom to assess her appearance, she returned to the ballroom, gathered her belongings from the book signing, and strode straight to the hotel lobby where her luggage awaited her.

As she walked to the taxi line, Veronica called her name.

"Wait, Stacy!" The younger woman ran toward her. "You're not leaving, are you?"

"Yes, I am. It was great meeting you, Ronnie. Be sure to send me your work to critique. I'll be happy to help."

Veronica paused to catch her breath. "I've got to start working out."

"You look great."

"Yeah, but I'm in lousy shape. Don't leave yet. I need to talk to you."

"What is it? I only have a few minutes. There's a flight I want to catch on standby."

"I need to talk to you about Michael."

"Look, Ronnie, I don't blame you for what happened. Or Dino. In fact, I'm glad I found out."

"I know, Stacy. I know you don't blame us. Though I feel awful about it."

"Don't."

"It's just, Dino told me some more stuff about Michael. Stuff you should probably know."

"I know all about Michael Moretti that I need to know. He used me. Case closed."

"Stacy, please listen. He hasn't had an easy life."

"Who has?" Stacy shook her head. "I've really got to go, Ronnie. I don't want to miss this plane." She gave Veronica a quick hug. "Keep in touch."

Before Veronica could say anymore, Stacy lugged her suitcase outside and entered a waiting cab. Veronica rushed out the door as the cabbie drove off.

Home.

Home in her own bed would be the perfect spot for one last cry over Michael Moretti. Then she'd move on.

CHAPTER NINE

Freaking tears again.

Stacy sniffed. She'd been home for three weeks, and still she was crying rivers over Michael Moretti. How had this happened? Her work lay unfinished on the computer. Luckily, she didn't have any pressing deadlines to worry about, but normally, she prided herself on writing at least one thousand words every day, usually much more. She hadn't written more than a couple of hundred since she got home.

Time to suck it up, Oppenheimer.

She could get something out of this, use her experience for her next installment in the Starr Shannon urban fantasy series. The beauty of urban fantasy was that she didn't need a happy ending every time, and Starr could have a new love interest for each book. Stacy would take Mary's advice and make Starr a cougar this time, give her a younger lover. Starr was thirty-nine, so her lover could be thirty or younger. Twenty-nine, Stacy thought, was a good age for her hero. Her sex with Michael could serve as the basis for the sex scenes. Stacy smiled to herself. This time she wouldn't have to guess what an orgasm felt like.

Now, some research on cougar and cub relationships. She sat at her computer and starting typing into her search engine. Over a million hits! Well, starting at the beginning would work well, she guessed. She scanned the pages...perfect! The Cougar Club offered advice and, better yet, a chatroom! What better place to research than with real live cougars?

And she could stay anonymous. She registered with a screen name, StacyStarr, and logged in.

HollyGolightly: *Hi, Stacy!*

MrsRobinson: *Hi there, Stacy!*

StacyStarr: *Hello*

MrsRobinson: *What brings you out tonight?*

Stacy inhaled. What should she say? Should she be honest that she was a writer doing research? Yes, that would probably be best. But perhaps the other women wouldn't appreciate being asked questions?

No, honesty was best.

StacyStarr: *I'm a writer. Do you mind if I ask you some questions?*

HollyGolightly: *Of course not.*

MrsRobinson: *Go right ahead. Or go "write" ahead, lol.*

HollyGolightly: *Lol, Megan.*

Geez, had these women been drinking? But they seemed open to her quest for information, so she dived in.

StacyStarr: *I was wondering, I guess, what*

younger men see in older women?

HollyGolightly: *There's not really an easy answer to that question, Stacy. Stacy is your name, right?*

StacyStarr: *Yes, my name is Stacy.*

HollyGolightly: *My guy and I met on a one-night stand, to be honest. I was in a bad place, and he really helped. I never meant to see him again, but we found each other later, and the connection was still there.*

MrsRobinson: *Holly's right. Honestly, most cougar/cub relationships that I know of began with a connection, not with any conscious thought on the woman's part to go after a younger man or on the man's part to go after an older woman.*

Hmmm. Interesting.

MrsRobinson: *I wasn't consciously looking for a cub either. I got lucky in that I found a man, who happened to be younger, who wasn't interested in having children. He's a great stepdad to my two daughters.*

Sheesh. Stacy hadn't even considered the kid issue. Michael was nearly ten years younger than she. Surely he would want kids. Stacy had wanted kids at one time, but it hadn't happened with David, and now she figured she was too old. Only months away from her forty-sixth birthday. Perimenopause could set in any day now. Yes, she'd wanted to be a mother at one time, but now? She wasn't so sure she could do it.

But...

Oh, God.

It had been three weeks since the writers' conference. When had she had her last period? She did some quick mental calculations. It had come well before the conference, and she hadn't had one since. She'd stopped keeping track during her marriage to David. Though they'd had their sterile sex regularly, she'd never gotten pregnant. She'd assumed after a while that she was sterile.

Oh, God again.

Could David have been the sterile one?

Of course not. She was sterile. And even if she wasn't, Michael had used a rubber each time. She was obviously worrying over nothing. For crying out loud, at her age, she was bound to start getting irregular. And who knew what regular was? She hadn't been keeping track anyway.

MrsRobinson: *Are you still there, Stacy?*

She jolted back to reality.

StacyStarr: *Yeah, I'm here.*

Here and freaking out.

StacyStarr: *How many of you cougars are*

there on this site?

MrsRobinson: *Quite a few of us. Simone and Katelyn are the two women who started the site. They're here quite a bit. Not sure where they are tonight.*

HollyGolightly: *Simone's out of town. I don't know where Katelyn is. But we have over five hundred women registered on the site now, and we get over 10,000 hits every day.*

> **StacyStarr:** *Wow. That's amazing. And all these relationships started without any conscious thought of age?*

MrsRobinson: *Of course we can't speak for all of them. Simone, for example, has always loved younger men and looks for them. But most of them seem to have started without any thought to age.*

> **StacyStarr:** *I find that very interesting.*

MrsRobinson: *Why?*

> **StacyStarr:** *Well, I guess because it seems like those types of relationships could go the same way as the older man/younger woman relationships. You know, when a young woman is looking for a sugar daddy?*

MrsRobinson: *Of course that's possible. But I don't know of any relationships on this site* *that are like that.*

> **StacyStarr:** *I guess I don't see why a younger man would want an older woman then, unless he was looking for a sugar mama.*

HollyGolightly: *Stacy, can I ask you something?*

> **StacyStarr:** *Of course.*

HollyGolightly: *We're not talking about research any more, are we?*

Warmth crept into Stacy's cheeks. How did they know?

> **StacyStarr:** *No. We're not.*

HollyGolightly: *You want to tell us what happened?*

Yes, she wanted to tell them. She had to tell someone, and here, veiled by a computer screen, perhaps she'd be comfortable speaking her mind. She started pouring out the story, and as she typed, an anvil lifted from her shoulders. Nothing would change, but damn, if felt good to talk about it.

MrsRobinson: *And you haven't had any contact with Michael since?*

> **StacyStarr:** *No. I haven't contacted him. And he hasn't tried to contact me, to my knowledge.*

MrsRobinson: *How do you know? Maybe he's tried and he hasn't been able to.*

> **StacyStarr:** *I told you I'm a writer. He knows my pen name. He can easily find my contact information on the web.*

Typing the words pierced Stacy's heart. He hadn't contacted her. He hadn't cared enough to try.

HollyGolightly: *She has a point, Megan.*

MrsRobinson: *But still, if you were only a sugar mama candidate, why did he come after you? Why did he make love to you that last time?*

> **StacyStarr:** *It wasn't lovemaking. It was a fuck, pure and simple. And I was a fool to allow it to happen.*

MrsRobinson: *You're not a fool if you were following your heart.*

> **StacyStarr:** *But I was a fool. I didn't mean to develop feelings. It was supposed to be a fun conference fling with a hot calendar boy. Nothing more. I never thought it would mean more to him, either. I just never expected...*

MrsRobinson: *You never expected to fall in love.*

StacyStarr: *NO*

She hammered the letters onto the keyboard.

StacyStarr: *I'm not in love with him.
I'm just hurt, you know? He only wanted
a sugar mama.*

HollyGolightly: *So you'd rather he's just
thought of you as a one-night stand?*

Would she?

StacyStarr: *Oh, hell. I don't know what I'd
rather he thought, to be honest.*

HollyGolightly: *Only you know what you're
feeling, Stacy, but I think Megan might be
right. You're feeling something more for this
man, or you wouldn't be hurting so much over
his betrayal. You'd be over it by now.*

StacyStarr: *I really AM doing research for a
cougar story.*

She added a smiley emoticon.

HollyGolightly: *Lol, we believe you, don't we,
Megan?*

MrsRobinson: *Of course we do. And I want
to read your story when it's done. But if we can*

help with your relationship problem too, all the better.

> **StacyStarr:** *That's a bit of a misnomer. Michael and I don't have a relationship.*

MrsRobinson: *Here's what we know, Stacy. One, he was looking for a sugar mama. Two, he made love to you and took you sky diving and changed your life for the better by helping you overcome your introversion. Three, when you found out he was looking for a sugar mama, you threw him out. Four, he came back to you, made love to you again. Five, you told him to leave you alone. And six, he has since left you alone. Those are the facts, right?*

> **StacyStarr:** *Yes, that sums it up.*

MrsRobinson: *I think, then, the next step is up to you.*

> **StacyStarr:** *What do you mean?*

MrsRobinson: *Well, he came back to you after you threw him out, made love to you, tried to talk to you, but you sent him packing again. So the ball's in your court now.*

> **StacyStarr:** *You think I should contact him?*

MrsRobinson: *It's been what, three weeks? And you're still thinking about him, right?*

Was she ever! To the detriment of her work too.

StacyStarr: *Yes, that's true.*

MrsRobinson: *Then contact him. Hear him out. Maybe his friend misunderstood what he was looking for. Or maybe he didn't but Michael has his own explanation. Or maybe he developed feelings for you.*

StacyStarr: *I doubt it.*

MrsRobinson: *Why would you doubt it? You didn't mean to develop feelings for him, but you did. Why couldn't he have done the same? Don't you owe it to yourself to find out?*

StacyStarr: *I'm not sure. I could end up feeling worse than I do now.*

HollyGolightly: *Or you could end up feeling better.*

MrsRobinson: *And do you really think you could feel any worse?*

True enough. She was already miserable. The worst thing that could happen was that she'd still be miserable.

StacyStarr: *Thank you. To both of you. Maybe I'll try to contact him. I can promise I'll think about it.*

MrsRobinson: *Good for you!*

> **StacyStarr:** *I need to get going. But I really do want to do some research on cougar/cub relationships too. Do you mind if I come back sometime?*

HollyGolightly: *Of course not! Everyone is welcome here.*

> **StacyStarr:** *Thanks! I'm really glad I found you guys. Talk to you soon!*

Stacy logged out of the chatroom and pulled up Michael's website. No doubt about it, the man was a god. Head shots, body shots, shots with gorgeous female models, book covers—everything on the site made her drool. Had always made her drool. She tensed when she got to the black-and-white shower shot she adored—the shot from the calendar that she'd been ogling when she first met Michael.

Seeing Michael dripping with water brought back pleasant memories that stung her heart. The pleasure of their wet and soapy bodies sliding together, his strong fingers shampooing her hair, his hard cock sliding in and out of her slick heat while droplets of water pelted her face and shoulders...

No.

She jolted back to reality. Her mouse hovered above the "Contact Michael" link.

She shook her head. She couldn't do it. Megan and Holly were no doubt right—she should find out once and for all where Michael stood. But her fear slithered up her spine, threatening to choke her.

She'd been rejected once before. She wasn't sure she could take it again. So much for only being as miserable as she was now.

Instead of contacting Michael, she typed his name into the search engine. Why not make herself more miserable by surfing the web and fnding out everything possible about the man she loved?

For she did love him. Admitting it produced a strange mixture of elation and sorrow in her heart. A connection to Michael pierced her soul with a fierce need and desire that she'd never felt for David or any other man.

True love.

She'd finally found it, finally felt it.

Too bad it would never be returned.

She surfed through web page after web page honoring the work and image of Michael Moretti. The Chicago Playboys site boasted what seemed like hundreds of photos of Michael holding adoring females on his lap, sometimes two and three at a time, of Michael kissing said adoring females, of said adoring females touching Michael's sculpted torso or the bulge beneath his tight black pants.

Sadness surged through Stacy. Michael was no doubt back on the road now, performing for these salivating females. He could sleep with any one of them. Hell, he probably was sleeping with them. How many women had he been with since her?

A shallow breath left her body. Pinpricks skittered over her flesh. Damn him! Damn Michael Moretti for making her feel so alive! And then taking it away...

Still, she continued the self-flagellation of surfing through each web page associated with Michael Moretti. Like the hundreds of people in cars on the highway who can't help gawking at an accident on the side of the road, she couldn't help looking at page after page of Michael.

Michael doing a cover shoot, Michael being interviewed on a romance author's blog, Michael participating in a charity bachelor auction, Michael mourning the death of his fiancée...

What?

Stacy widened her eyes. On her computer screen was a grainy black-and-white photo of a much younger Michael Moretti, nine years younger to be exact. He had just started shooting covers, had just started making a name for himself in the business. The article was from a local newspaper and had obviously been scanned onto the computer by the owner of this particular fan page. Stacy squinted to read the small blurry print.

CHAPTER TEN

"You not eating enough." Michael's mother heaped spaghetti and meatballs onto his plate. "You going to waste away, Michele."

Michele. *Mee-kay-lay.* Only his mother used his given Italian first name. He'd changed it in elementary school when the boys had realized it spelled a girl's name in English. After a bloodied nose and black eye, he'd had enough.

Francesca Moretti prepared the best spaghetti and meatballs in all of Chicago, in all the world, probably, but today, they tasted like sawdust to Michael.

"I've only lost a few pounds, Ma."

"That's not like you. Now eat." She shoved the plate closer to him.

He twirled spaghetti on his fork and brought it to his lips. Yep, still sawdust.

"Now, you tell me what's wrong," his mother said, sitting next to him.

"Nothing's wrong."

"When my son lose weight and no eat my spaghetti, something's wrong."

Michael regarded his mother, a little plump now, but still a beautiful woman at sixty years old. He'd never understood why his father had left. Once grown, Michael had helped her out as much as he could. His whole sugar mama idea had been as much for his mother as it was for him. Once he was too old to dance and model, how would he make a living? How would he help take care of her?

"You spend two days at home and no eat."

He took another bite of spaghetti. "I'm eating."

"Why you not on the road?"

"I took some time off. They're training a few new guys and they didn't need me right now."

Truth was, the new blood was younger, buffer, and hotter. Michael had overheard one of the managers commenting on his love handles. So losing a few pounds was a good thing. Hell, he hadn't even been trying.

"You meet a girl, Michele?"

A girl. Was this really all about a girl? Stacy still haunted his mind. All he'd wanted was a woman who would take care of him in exchange for his companionship. Should it have been that difficult to find? It wasn't like he was broke. He had some savings. He even had a small house. He'd had relationships here and there, but never anything permanent, never anything real.

Not like what he'd had with Beth.

No, he wasn't looking for that. Love meant heartache. First, his father abandoned him, and then Beth.

Nope, never again.

"You know how I feel about women, Ma."

"Yes, I know you like women, just don't want to marry one."

"Is there anything wrong with that?"

"You getting old, Michele. Where my grandbabies?"

"Getting old! Damn it, Ma, I hear that every day in the industry I'm in. I don't need to hear it from you."

"Don't you use that language with me, Michele."

"I'm sorry, Ma. I truly am." There went the Catholic guilt again. No one got to Michael like his mother did. "But you asked me where your grandbabies are. You know the answer to that. Your grandbaby is in the ground. With Beth."

"I know you love Beth." His mother smiled, and the tiny wrinkles around her dark eyes softened. "I love Beth too. And that baby she carry. But that long time ago, Michele. Time to heal."

"Like you healed? You never got over Dad leaving."

His mother's dark eyes sank, her lashes fluttered closed. "Your papa leave me and you. He young, strong, and healthy, and he leave and never come back." She opened her eyes, locked her gaze with his. "Beth no leave you."

"The hell she didn't."

"She die, Michele. She no leave on purpose."

He knew that. But still her memory pierced his heart. Their child would be eight years old now. He often wondered whether he'd have a son or a daughter, whether he or she would have Beth's soft blue eyes, his thick dark hair.

"I see the look in your eyes, Michele. The sadness, the love. I not see that since Beth die."

He scoffed and twirled more tasteless spaghetti around his fork. "You're seeing things, Ma."

"I know my son. I know what I see."

Michael shook his head. He could deny it no longer. Stacy had gotten under his skin, into his heart, and into his soul.

"Okay. There's a woman."

"I know."

"She's a writer. I met her at that conference I went to a few weeks ago."

"What's her name?"

"Stacy."

"She not love you back?"

"No. And I can't blame her. I made some stupid mistakes. I thought...I thought I knew what I wanted. I went there looking for a woman."

"Then what's the problem?"

"I said I went there looking for a woman. I just didn't bank on finding someone I cared about so much."

"Why you look for a woman if you not want to care?"

He let out a breath he hadn't realized he'd been holding. He could never explain the sugar mama concept to his mother. She wouldn't understand. Hell, he no longer understood. What had he been thinking? He was many things, but a user of women had never been one of them. He'd been a womanizer after Beth, yes, but the women he bedded had always gotten what they wanted.

Getting old in an industry that focused on the young sometimes led to desperation. He'd seen it before. Too bad he hadn't recognized it in himself. But hell, was he any less desperate now? His appetite was nearly nonexistent, and he'd been whacking off like an adolescent to Stacy's image in his memory since the conference.

If only he could go back, do it all over...

But would he have met Stacy otherwise, if he hadn't been searching for an older woman who might be willing to take care of him?

No, he wouldn't have. He wouldn't have been looking for a woman at all. He would have made do with the scads of women who threw themselves at him, who meant nothing to him.

Stacy wouldn't have been one of them. She was too shy, too inhibited.

Aw, hell no. She'd proved she could get over that. She wouldn't have thrown herself at him because she had too much class. That's the kind of woman she was. Classy. Like his mother. Like Beth.

"You going to answer me?"

"Sorry, Ma. I went looking for a woman for all the wrong reasons. I see that now."

"And what you find?"

"I found someone amazing. Someone who lights up my world."

"Tell me about her."

"She's beautiful, and smart. She's amazing. She's older than I am."

"How old?"

"Forty-five."

"So what? That still young enough to give me grandbabies."

Michael couldn't help but chuckle. "You do have a one track mind, Ma."

"Michele"—she scooted her chair closer to him, cupped both his cheeks in her soft hands—"as much as I want grandbabies, I want you happy more. If this woman can make you happy, I don't care if she a hundred years old. Can this woman make you happy?"

"I think so, yes."

"Why you not with her then?"

"I screwed it up."

"Then fix it."

He chuckled. If only if were that simple. "I don't think it can be fixed, Ma. I tried."

"You love her?"

He closed his eyes, gripped the edge of the table. "Yes," he said, his heart opening, freeing what he'd locked inside for so long, since Beth had died. "I love her."

God, how he loved her. Her incredible big brown eyes, her silky auburn hair. He loved her shyness, yet how her inhibitions seemed to cease to exist at opportune times, like when she'd told him her breasts were real the first time they met. He loved how she'd fought him tooth and nail about sky diving but then how her face had lit up as she'd described the experience later. He loved how she kissed him, how she'd painted his hard cock with chocolate sauce and then licked it all off in the best blow job of his life. He loved how perfectly she fit into his arms when they danced, when they showered, when they made love.

"I love her," he said again softly.

His mother touched his forearm, but her gentleness didn't extend to her face. Her features were taut, her lips pursed. "Try *harder.*"

CHAPTER ELEVEN

StacyStarr: *I found out something about Michael.*

HollyGolightly: *What?*

StacyStarr: *He had a fiancée. She died nine years ago in a car accident.*

HollyGolightly: *Oh, wow, that's awful.*

StacyStarr: *That's not even the worst of it. She was pregnant with his child.*

HollyGolightly: *I take it you haven't contacted him yet.*

StacyStarr: *No, I couldn't. Not after I read this. He adored this woman, this Beth. I could never take her place. I don't think I want to.*

HollyGolightly: *He's not the first person to lose a loved one. And it was a long time ago.*

StacyStarr: *But it makes sense now, why he's a womanizer. Even why he was looking for a sugar mama. He never got over Beth. I think* *he may be punishing women now. Punishing them for what he perceived as Beth's abandonment. I don't think he's ever going to let himself have feelings for a woman again.*

HollyGolightly: *You don't know that. You're making a lot of assumptions, Stacy.*

StacyStarr: *I know. But I'm afraid of rejection, Holly. What if he really only wants a sugar mama?*

HollyGolightly: *Remember that he tried to make up with you once already. You won't know until you ask.*

StacyStarr: *If he really wanted me, he'd come to me.*

HollyGolightly: *Not necessarily. He may be afraid of you rejecting him.*

Michael Moretti afraid of rejection? Was she kidding?

StacyStarr: *I don't think that's an issue. I guess I haven't given you his full name, but trust me, if you saw him, you'd know he would have no fear of rejection.*

HollyGolightly: *Stacy, good looking people have just as many insecurities as the rest of us, lol.*

StacyStarr: *He could have any woman he wanted.*

HollyGolightly: *Don't forget what you know about him now. He lost a fiancée he adored along with an unborn child. That can devastate a person. You said yourself that he adored her. It was a long time ago, and he might be ready to open his heart again to the right woman. But it's been a long time, and you've already rejected him once.*

StacyStarr: *I suppose...*

HollyGolightly: *It's true. You rejected him.*

StacyStarr: *But only after he rejected me. I mean, I guess he didn't technically reject me.*

HollyGolightly: *No, he didn't. And when you found out why he'd gone after you in the first place, he tried to make it up to you.*

StacyStarr: *You think so?*

HollyGolightly: *Based on what you've told me, yes, I think so.*

StacyStarr: *Maybe...*

HollyGolightly: *Have I convinced you to contact him yet?*

StacyStarr: *I think so. Yes.*

HollyGolightly: *Good! I hope it works out for you. Promise you'll get back online and let us know, okay?*

StacyStarr: *I will. I definitely will! Thank you, Holly!*

Stacy logged off, elation filling her, and surfed straight to Michael's official website. This time she didn't let the mouse hover over the "Contact Michael" link. She clicked, and an email form popped up.

"Dear Michael," she wrote, "I hope this finds you well. I've been thinking about you and the time we shared at the conference. I'd like to talk to you if you're still willing. I think we both left a lot of things unsaid. You can reach me at this email address. Take care, Stacy."

Perhaps she'd hear from him, perhaps she wouldn't, but one thing was for certain—after hitting "send" she felt better than she had in days. At least she'd done something, been proactive.

Right now, she couldn't get Michael's hard body and thick cock out of her head. He'd given her her first orgasm. Her body longed to fly again.

She smiled to herself. After her divorce from David, she'd swallowed her inhibitions for about five minutes and strode into a sex shop on the other side of town. There she'd purchased a vibrator and some lube, hoping she'd be able to produce an orgasm. Though she'd managed to pay for the items and leave the store without fainting or vomiting, once she'd returned home, she hadn't had had the nerve to try them.

She had the nerve now. This was something even Starr

Shannon had not done.

Stacy's nipples tightened at the thought. She shed her clothes quickly, opened the bottom drawer of her dresser where she'd hidden her toys underneath her long underwear, and pulled them out. The vibrator, still encased in plastic, shone a hot pink.

Hot pink!

Why did manufacturers choose such strange and vibrant colors? Right now, though, the toy no longer looked like the menace it had seemed when she first plunked it into the bottom of the drawer over a year ago. No, now it looked like a plaything, a bauble, a colorful treasure that could produce pleasure for her until Michael Moretti came back to her bed.

And if he didn't? Her heart slacked a little. She'd miss him, yes. But there were other fish in the sea. She'd find someone else worthy with whom to share her newfound sexual prowess.

Stacy Oppenheimer would not be alone forever, and neither would she enter another passionless relationship. Twenty years she had wasted with David! But time was still on her side. Forty-five was a long way from dead.

She discarded the plastic packaging, inserted the batteries, and fingered the silicone toy. Soft and pliable, it was warm to her touch. Just the thought of her impending orgasm made her drip.

She lay down on her rumpled bed. Her nipples seemed a good place to start. They were already taut and hard, and just the brush of her fingers over them made her squirm. Tiny sparks skittered across her flesh. She plucked at each turgid nipple, twisted, pinched, until she had to leave one breast to rub the erect nub of her clit.

Her folds were slick with nectar, and she dipped a finger

into her moisture and smoothed it over her clit, circling, teasing, until...oh! She hit just the right spot. Time for the vibrator. Stacy was so wet she didn't need the lube. Though taking her free hand from her breast left her nipple aching, it paled in comparison to the throbbing inside her wet tunnel. She needed to be filled. Now.

She gently eased the pink phallus into her pussy while she continued to manipulate her clit. In and out, thrust and thrust—faster she went. She closed her eyes and visualized Michael's thick cock tunneling in and out of her, slowly at first, easily, and then gaining momentum until he was pounding into her with every thrust. Tension built within her, until her entire body burned with a blistering fever. Perspiration covered her molten flesh. Still in and out she plunged, the vibrator humming as she continued her self-pleasure. She twirled her fingers over her swollen clit until the intensity reached the highest peak, and she burst.

Electrifying embers shot through her, radiating outward, taking her to the summit she had only recently discovered. Her own moans and wails filled the room, seemed to float from the ceiling and down the walls, until she drifted downward and landed on her soft mattress.

Wow.

To think she'd gone all the adult years of her life without this feeling of exhilaration, of escape, of pure joy and satisfaction. She sighed and smiled to herself. Starr would definitely be having a masturbatory orgasm in Stacy's next book.

As wonderful as her self-produced orgasm had been, though, it paled to what she'd experienced in Michael's arms.

No use crying over what might not be, and no use sitting

around waiting for him to return her email. What she needed was exercise. She'd become quite a slouch, sitting around the townhome doing nothing but crying, eating, crying some more. Those days were over. She hadn't run since before the conference, and her body was feeling the loss. She went to the sink and washed her private parts and then her toy, put it away, and put on some fresh jogging clothes. After tying her long hair into a ponytail, she smiled to herself. The sun shone brightly and the temperature hovered around seventy degrees—perfect running weather.

She locked the door, hooked her house key to her jogging pants, and started at a steady pace to the park where she jogged regularly.

The sunshine warmed her skin, the sweet scent of fresh flowers permeated her as she inhaled. She had missed this, missed running.

She turned the corner of the street that would lead her to the park. She looked up at the cerulean sky. Such a beautiful day, such a beautiful world.

Her neck jerked at the shrill shriek of tires skidding.

Then a thousand knives cut into her body as her head thudded onto the cement. *Crack*... Blackness enshrouded her.

★ ★ ★

Michael stood nervously on the cement doorstep of Stacy's townhome. She'd emailed him, so she must still care. He'd returned the email as soon as he'd received it two days ago.

Then...nothing.

Was this some sort of cruel joke?

He'd called in a favor to his cousin, a private investigator, who'd helped him uncover Stacy's real last name—Oppenheimer—and her address in a Chicago suburb. Lucky for him, she didn't live far. They'd both flown to the conference in Denver.

He took a deep breath and knocked on the door.

A man answered.

Oh, shit.

He was nice looking, tall with graying dark hair, dressed in jeans and a t-shirt. Was he Stacy's boyfriend?

"I'm looking for Stacy Summers...Oppenheimer."

"Are you a friend of hers?" the man asked.

Michael cleared his throat. "Yes. Is she here?"

"I guess you haven't heard," the man said. "I'm Kevin McNeal, Stacy's neighbor. Come on in."

Heard what? Michael stepped inside. "What's going on? Is she okay?"

"So far, she seems to be. It's still up in the air."

Michael's heart plummeted to his stomach. "Oh my God."

"As you probably know, Stacy doesn't have any immediate family living."

Michael nodded.

"She carries my name and number in her wallet as her emergency contact information. Two days ago, she was hit by a car while she was out jogging. The jerk didn't even stop."

"Oh, God." Nausea rumbled in the pit of his stomach. Beth all over again.

"She's alive. And out of ICU as of this morning, thank God."

ICU? "Is she conscious?"

"Yes. I talked to her a little earlier today. But they have her pretty sedated. She's got a broken arm and collar bone and contusions all over her body. She's lucky more bones aren't broken. She had some internal bleeding in the stomach and intestines. That's why she was in ICU. But that's been resolved."

"Thank God."

"Oh, and there's more good news."

Good news? His heart rejoiced. "What?"

"So far she hasn't lost the baby."

CHAPTER TWELVE

Baby?

Michael nearly lost his footing. Stacy was pregnant?

It couldn't be his. They'd used protection.

Damn her! She'd written him, made him believe there was a chance, when all this time...

No. He willed his mind to settle. It didn't matter. What mattered was that she was all right. That she was alive.

Stacy was alive, not dead like Beth. God damn it, Michael would see that she stayed alive. If she carried another man's child, they would deal with it.

"You look surprised," Kevin said.

"Yes. I didn't know she was pregnant."

"Neither did I. We've been pretty good friends since she moved in here after her divorce, but I didn't even know she was seeing anyone."

Damn. If her friend and neighbor—the man who was her emergency contact—didn't know she was seeing anyone... Could it be?

Condoms weren't one hundred percent effective, but he didn't remember one breaking. Of course, he hadn't looked carefully either, and they'd gone at it harshly at times. Despite the situation, he smiled faintly at the memory.

"She isn't very far along," Kevin went on. "The ER doctors detected a faint fetal heartbeat when she was initially brought in. They told me at first that she'd most likely lose the child.

When she didn't, they said it was pretty much a medical miracle."

No shit. A fucking miracle. A wonderful baby who was trying desperately to enter this world despite condoms and hit and run drivers.

God, the baby had to be his. It *had* to be.

A beautiful baby with the woman he loved—it was a dream he'd thought long dead.

"I'll take you over there if you like," Kevin said, "I'm going myself."

"I'll follow you," Michael said. "I don't plan to leave until she does."

"Oh." Kevin's eyes widened. "You're not...?"

"The father of the baby?" Suddenly, it didn't matter whether he was the biological father or not. That baby was his. His and Stacy's. The need to take care of both of them enveloped him in a thick haze. "Yes, I am."

"Wow. Let's get over there then. I'm sure she'll be thrilled to see you."

Michael's heart raced until the moment he stood outside Stacy's room. His Stacy lay in the bed, one eye swollen shut, the other open and alert as a nurse held a strange instrument over her abdomen.

"That's a Doppler," Kevin said. "She's checking the baby's heartbeat."

A rapid staccato sounded from the device. "Is it supposed to be that fast?"

The nurse turned around. "Yes," she said. "It's supposed to be that fast. Baby is nice and healthy so far. Hello, Kevin."

"Hello," Kevin said. "This is Michael, another friend of Stacy's."

Stacy's head jerked forward a little.

"Michael?" Her voice was soft and raspy.

"Yeah, baby, I'm here," Michael said, his heart pounding. "Can I come in?"

The nurse looked at Stacy, and Stacy nodded.

"Just for a little while," the nurse said. "Stacy needs her rest."

Kevin excused himself and left. The room smelled sterile when Michael inhaled. No flowers graced the surroundings. He'd remedy that as soon as possible. He pulled up a chair and sat next to the bed.

"You look beautiful."

She winced. "Don't make me laugh, Michael. It hurts."

"God! I'm sorry."

"Did you get my email?"

"Yeah. I emailed you back, and when you didn't respond, I came here looking for you. I'm so sorry about all this, Stace."

"This? This isn't your fault."

"I know. But if I'd had half a brain, we would have been together long before now, and maybe this wouldn't have happened."

"There's no way to know that for sure. I'm going to be all right. I got really lucky."

"Thank God. If something had happened to you..." Michael swallowed. "I can't lose you, baby. I...I love you."

"Oh, Michael!" She reached for him but grimaced in pain.

Michael's heart broke to see her like this. "Don't try to move, sweetheart." He leaned toward her. "I'll come to you." He touched his mouth softly to hers. Her full red lips were parched and dry.

"Michael, do you really?"

"Yes, baby. I love you. I'm so sorry about everything. I thought I wanted a woman to take care of me. I thought I could live without love. But I can't, not now that I've found you."

"I should have listened to you at the conference."

"No, Stace. No. You bear no blame here. It's all on me." He meant it. "I'm so sorry."

"It's okay. I'm just so glad you're here now." She closed her open eye, and a tear squeezed out. "Michael, I know about Beth."

"I know. Dino told Ronnie."

"Ronnie didn't tell me. I haven't talked to her since the conference. I found an old article online. I'm so sorry that you lost her and your child."

"It was a long time ago."

"But it still hurts."

"Yes, it still hurts. But I found another woman I love more than life itself. If she'll have me?"

His heart skittered as he awaited her answer.

"I will have you, Michael. I love you too."

Joy filled him. She loved him!

"Michael, I have to tell you something."

"What, baby?"

"It's a miracle. We...we're going to have a baby."

"So it *is* mine?"

"You know?"

"Kevin told me. I don't think he thought it was a secret, so don't get mad at him."

"I'm not mad at him, and yes, of course it's yours. I had no idea. I thought I was infertile, and you used condoms. But I haven't been with anyone else. It has to be yours."

A primal desire to run to the top of a mountain and roar

surged through Michael. The woman he loved carried his child.

"Listen, baby," he said, pushing her hair off her moist brow. "You need to take care of yourself. I'm not leaving your side. We need to get you healed up good as new, okay?"

"Yes, I can do it, now that you're here. I can do it for you and our baby."

"I know you can. God, I love you so much. As soon as you're all better, will you do something for me?"

"Anything, Michael."

He smiled. "Will you marry me?"

"Yes," she said, and the look on her face made his heart melt. "Yes, Michael, I will marry you."

★ ★ ★

Seven months later

"Had enough?" Michael eased the baby from Stacy's arms and set him in the bassinet next to Stacy's hospital bed.

Stacy smiled. "That baby sure knows how to eat for only being a little over twenty-four hours old."

"I can certainly understand that." Michael leaned down and kissed Stacy's cheek. "I can't resist those breasts of yours either. They were the first thing I noticed about you, remember?"

Warmth crept up Stacy's neck as the memory emerged. Michael, dressed in jeans and a white shirt, looking like the male model he was, ogling her chest and saying "that's a nice shirt." How far they'd come since then, but Stacy wouldn't change a minute of their time together. They'd been married six months and still her husband could make her blush. She hoped that never changed.

"Hey. Can you hand me the laptop? There's something I need to do."

"No working, baby. I thought we agreed you're taking some time off. Now that I'm managing the Chicago Playboys, you can ease up on the writing."

Michael was proving to be great at his new job, a real asset to the male revue. "See? With your talent and intelligence, you never needed a sugar mama."

"I still got the woman I wanted though." He reached for the laptop. "What do you want this for? I'm serious about you not working. You just gave birth, for God's sake."

"I'm not going to work." Exhaustion overwhelmed her, but it paled in comparison to her deep happiness and contentment. "But there are some people who are waiting to hear the good news."

Michael set the laptop on her lap. Stacy fired it up and logged into the Cougar Club.

StacyStarr: *It's a boy!*

MESSAGE FROM HELEN HARDT

Dear Reader,

Thank you for reading *Cougar Chronicles*. If you want to find out about my current backlist and future releases, please like my Facebook page and join my mailing list. I often do giveaways. If you're a fan and would like to join my street team to help spread the word about my books. I regularly do awesome giveaways for my street team members.

If you enjoyed the story, please take the time to leave a review on a site like Amazon or Goodreads. I welcome all feedback. I wish you all the best!

Helen

Facebook
Facebook.com/HelenHardt

Newsletter
HelenHardt.com/SignUp

Street Team
Facebook.com/Groups/HardtAndSoul

ALSO BY HELEN HARDT

Cougar Chronicles:
The Cowboy and the Cougar
Calendar Boy

The Steel Brothers Saga:
Craving
Obsession
Possession
Melt
Burn
Surrender
Shattered
Twisted
Unraveled
Breathless
Ravenous
Insatiable (Coming Soon)

Blood Bond Saga:
Unchained
Unhinged
Undaunted
Unmasked
Undefeated

Misadventures Series:
Misadventures with a Rock Star
Misadventures of a Good Wife (with Meredith Wild)

The Temptation Saga:
Tempting Dusty
Teasing Annie
Taking Catie
Taming Angelina
Treasuring Amber
Trusting Sydney
Tantalizing Maria

The Sex and the Season Series:
Lily and the Duke
Rose in Bloom
Lady Alexandra's Lover
Sophie's Voice

Daughters of the Prairie:
The Outlaw's Angel
Lessons of the Heart
Song of the Raven

ACKNOWLEDGMENTS

Thank you to my good friend Lizzie T. Leaf for first convincing me to write a cougar story. It was fun and challenging! Thank you to Celina Summers for your skillful editing. Your red pen is one of the toughest I've encountered. It's always an honor to work with you.

Thank to everyone at Waterhouse Press—Meredith, David, Jon, Shayla, Kurt, Yvonne—for bringing the cougars and their cubs back to life.

And of course to my street team members, family and friends, and readers—thank you for your unending support. It means more than you know.

ABOUT THE AUTHOR

#1 *New York Times*, #1 *USA Today*, and #1 *Wall Street Journal* bestselling author Helen Hardt's passion for the written word began with the books her mother read to her at bedtime. She wrote her first story at age six and hasn't stopped since. In addition to being an award-winning author of romantic fiction, she's a mother, an attorney, a black belt in Taekwondo, a grammar geek, an appreciator of fine red wine, and a lover of Ben and Jerry's ice cream. She writes from her home in Colorado, where she lives with her family. Helen loves to hear from readers.

Visit her at HelenHardt.com

ALSO AVAILABLE FROM
HELEN HARDT

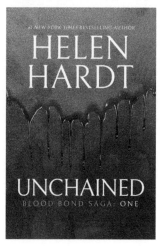

Dante Gabriel is starving. What he craves is red gold—human blood. After being held captive as a blood slave to a female vampire for years, he has finally escaped. Unchained at last, he follows his nose to the nearest blood bank to sate his hunger.

ER nurse Erin Hamilton expects just another busy night shift... until she finds a gorgeous stranger vandalizing the hospital blood bank. Though her logic tells her to turn him in, she's pulled by stronger and unfamiliar emotions to protect the man who seems oddly infatuated with her scent. Chemistry sizzles between them, but Dante, plagued by nightmares of his time in captivity, fears he won't be able to control himself...especially when he discovers a secret she doesn't even know she's hiding.

Visit HelenHardt.com for more information!